Kaoru's Chaos

Book Three of Vade Mecum

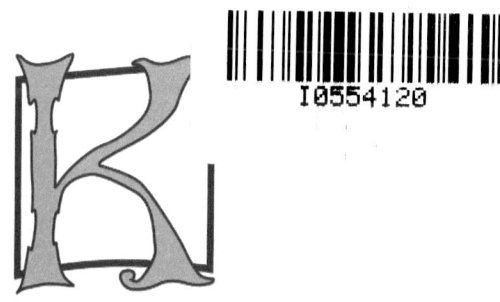

I0554120

By D.H. Dhaenens

Flammable Penguins Publishing

Table of Contents

First published in Great Britain in 2018 by FLAMMABLE PENGUINS PUBLISHING

ISBN 978-0-9956967-3-0

FLAMMABLE PENGUINS PUBLISHING
International House
24 Holborn Viaduct
CITY OF LONDON
London EC1A 2BN

www.flammablepenguins.com

To Claire, my shining star
To everyone who came along for this ride,
Thank you

Chapter 1

7 years ago

"I'm not going to say it!" Aiden laughed, looking over to Hayden as he held a hand out to help her off of the stage of the small venue. While it looked gloriously lush in the front, the back was almost circuslike, with straw littering the rough wooden floor.

Hayden looked to the floor hesitantly, and Aiden realised her ballet flats were too thin for this kind of terrain. He turned his back and moved his head.

"Come on. I'll piggy back you."

She climbed onto his back and kissed his cheek. "Alright. For that you can say it."

Aiden held back one second longer, pausing to adjust her on his back, then grinned.

"I told you they would love the tiger."

"It was your best yet." She acquiesced. "So what's next, grand demon summonings?"

"Don't even joke about that. That stuff is dangerous." Aiden had told her before about the limitations of his magic and the workings of it, as best he could. It was still new, but it was something he had grown up with for so long he had a pretty good idea of his abilities. It was also a handy way for him to earn money and be independent from any foster institutions. At seventeen he had run away from his last foster family. At nineteen he had gotten his first magic show, and now at twenty one he had a beautiful wife and a steady income from his shows.

Life couldn't get better than this. Sure, a few people in the blossoming magic community had been haughty to him, claiming it was wrong to use magic to earn money. They had clearly never been poor.

"I still can't believe we're going to Las Vegas." Hayden said with a grin. "We haven't been since the wedding."

"We will be working...But maybe we can get that nice honeymoon suite at last..." He peeked at her over his shoulder. Her hair bounced as they walked, big beautiful curls framing her freckled face. He still couldn't believe she had gone for someone like him. He still had zits, was gangly and his hair seemed to consist entirely of cowlicks. But he had a charm, he guessed. That's why people came to his shows.

He paused at the entrance to the dressing room. It was ajar when he was sure he locked it. He was very careful about the few props he'd managed to scrounge together over the years.

"Thieves?" She wiggled to be let down and he set her down carefully.

"I don' know. Stay here."Aiden breathed softly and opened the door wider. Fear gripped him – had someone broken in to try and steal their money? His heart bounded in his chest as he took a few steps to enter the dressing room. It all looked in order as he looked around.

Nobody. Maybe he had just forgotten to lock it? These things did happen. Just as he was about to turn to Hayden, he heard her cry out. A quick, pained yelp and she was no longer standing near him. As he turned he could just see her being slammed into the rough brick wall across the dressing room.

"Hayden!" He tried to close the distance but the dressing room door slammed in his face, hitting him in the nose.

"You keep playing with magic, boy." The woman looked angry, not much older than him. For a moment he wondered if she had been hiding behind the couch.

"You use it for selfish, petty purposes!"

"You touch Hayden again and I'll show you just what I can use my magic for!" He pulled open the door and closed the distance between him and Hayden. A second witch appeared just in front of him, keeping him from getting to her.

Hayden had regained herself a little and kicked at the witch's leg.

"What the fu-" She started. Unsurprisingly, her stockinged feet didn't do much damage. It looked like she had pissed off the woman more than anything. Where was security when you needed them? Probably too short staffed to be worried about the back of the house.

The witch picked Hayden up by her throat.
"All those who profit from magic will die." The first witch pushed Aiden to the side. "I thought we were going to kill the boy. But your death will set an example."
Aiden's head spinned as the first witch grabbed him. "No no no no no don't you fucking touch her! I - I'll stop - We'll stop using magic and-"
"And just run off somewhere else and do the same thing? Too little too late, kid." The second witch squeezed and he heard Hayden gasp for breath. The second witch was holding him back, using a spell to immobilise him. He could feel himself go limp.

"No! No no -" His body went completely limp and he slipped to the ground.
He could see Hayden's feet kick and then stop. In his mind the mantra kept going. No no no no. This couldn't be real.

His head was spinning. It felt like the air wasn't reaching his lungs. The darkness set in not long after.

Chapter 2

The doors to the conference centre opened up. A small crowd had been waiting outside the doors and staff was checking tickets and badges. There had been some networking and a speech from him yesterday, but this was the main event.

Day 2, Furcifer thought grimly. His faction, the Elites, had set this up. And although it was the first time they had organised anything remotely this big, but it seemed they were off to a good start. He was approached by a man carrying a lanyard with a big plastic badge on it.

"You'll need to wear-"

Furcifer side stepped him and kept walking into the main hall. No way was he going to wear some cheap lanyard with his name on his chest. What was next, carrying a giant placard that read "come hug me"?. He shook his head.

Aiden walked up to him, dressed smartly in a shirt, cardigan and dress pants – slightly more dressed up than normal. The only thing that looked strange on the man was the large conference badge clipped to his bag.

"They got you, huh?" He nodded at the badge.

Aiden shook his head with a chuckle. "Speaking of being had. I enjoyed your keynote speech yesterday." Aiden smirked.

Furcifer rolled his eyes. "Gabrielle forced me to." He did not enjoy large bouts of public speaking – especially a speech like yesterday which was basically a longer version of "thanks for coming, enjoy the booze".

"Still, it's a big deal to announce the first magic built monument at the first magical conference." Aiden insisted. "You didn't do too badly. Promise." He winked and looked around as others came in. Some had missed last night's opening speech and networking drinks, probably due to travel.

"All familiar faces." Aiden said before peeking at the programme.

"Aren't you doing a talk?"

"Potions and candles, the future of handmade magical items." He smiled. "It will be interesting to get some hands-on stuff with these people."

"I thought it was a talk?" Furcifer chuckled.

"Yes, but I want to make a potion with them as well. Make things memorable. Are you coming? It's right after your Magic and the Law round table. Gods,

Furcifer, that sounds pretentious."

Furcifer chuckled. "Don't tell me. We've had to make it into a very small meeting."

"You can say that again. I almost didn't make it in." He nodded to Ms Baxter who was just coming in. "And word is it's because of her."

"Pretty much. She almost didn't get in herself. I'm thinking she doesn't want you to work against her every step of the way."

"Then they shouldn't have killed my wife." He bristled and looked up. "Sorry."

"Did you have the dream again?" Furcifer asked softly. He knew the other had flashbacks, sometimes.

"It's the anniversary of her death tomorrow." He sighed. "Your talk is in fifteen minutes. Don't be late."

Furcifer nodded. "I'm sorry." He said, and for once he meant it.

Aiden hesitated, then nodded and took off.

In the end it was a good thing he had brought along Manon to help him out and had arrived fifteen minutes early, half expecting to relax for a while before people came in. Manon had told him to set up regardless, and it had been a good call. The laptop did not seem to work, until she pointed out he had not brought a power cord and had left the thing on most of the night. A quick rummage around later, they found an alternative, which then needed to be connected to the external display to show the slides. Luckily for Furcifer, he wasn't the first flummoxed professor she had helped out with a presentation. Manon also amused herself with the fact he tripped over the cord once or twice, not used to such level of tech in his own living quarters. Luckily, his audience had not seen it, and by the time they came in he had neatly finished his fumbling.

He looked over the list of names he had on his pad.
"Dear guests." He demanded the attention - they had come to hear him speak after all.
"Just a quick roll call. I'm seeing seven people on my list, but I'm counting 8?"
Muttering and people glancing around. It had been a battle to get into this round table as only faction leaders had been invited, initially. Only a few of those present did not have an entire squad of mages behind them.

"Joyce Baxter, Canutta coven?"

"Here!" A well-manicured hand shot up. Someone was paying attention.

"Hazel Glover, Witch faction?"

A muttering went up. Most of the attendees knew the Witches as conservatives, a reclusive sort, and after a secretive leadership switch everyone was curious about the new leader.

More timidly than Ms. Baxter, Hazel Glover put up her hand.

"That's me." She cleared her throat. Not the strong figure Furcifer had expected, but perhaps that was for the better.

"Mary Cobsworth, Scribes - ah yes. Glad you could join us."

Furcifer nodded to Mary, a fellow leader in his joint Elites-Scribe faction.

"Present. Also for the record, I am here to represent the Scribe faction, not my business interests."

Mary clarified, to the approving nods of many. All of them had some sort of business assets tied up in their factions, bur Mary's business was separate from the faction she lead, which worried some.

"Aiden Willemeens." Furcifer continued.

Aiden put his hand up.

"Twi - Asa Ward?" Force of habit of Furcifer's to refer to his friend by his nickname.

Aiden had to jab Twitch in the ribs before he put his hand up.

Furcifer ticked his own name off and scratched through the IMG leader's name. He had clearly not made it. The remaining two people stood up.

"Caught out I guess. Hi, everyone. My name is special agent Alexis White and this is my colleague Cecil Ellis. We're with the newly created magic bureau. We contacted you about attending."

Furcifer strained to think what was going on and how he should handle it.

"There was a lot of interest in this session, agent White, I'm sorry if I didn't get back to you."

"You did, with some choice expletives." Agent Ellis smiled serenely. Furcifer now remembered, and tried not to make a face. There had been an email from some strange government agency to attend the talks and his first instincts had been to sink that hope.

'But we were told to come so we came. I hope that's not an inconvenience. The government of this country is very much invested in the magic community after all."

Furcifer sighed. Of course the government would send representatives, even though he had mentioned these talks were just... preliminary, a talk among mages before others joined in. It seemed they were not allowed that privilege.

"Please continue." Ellis said, sitting down, and Furcifer realised angrily that he had let them take control of this interaction.

"Ah. Yes." He cleared his throat. "Welcome to this Magic and the Law Round Table. We'll be talking about the future of magic in conjunction with the current laws, and how the law framework will have to work around the magic capabilities the average user has. So I've prepared this round table to make sure we are all on the same page as to where we go next with this."

"What about the magic wave?" Joyce called out, and Furcifer worried she would try and derail the talks. Manon raised an eyebrow, but continued taking notes. Now he just hoped she wouldn't get snarky or this whole thing would derail. After a moment of silence, Furcifer spoke.

"I don't see the point in talking about those, ms Baxter, when we have no new information."

"There hasn't been a new wave of magic in years now, how do we know we're talking about something that will still be relevant ten years from now?"

Furcifer took in a deep breath.

"Ms Baxter. Rest assured. Just because no wave has hit

in a while does not mean there are no other mages to help out. Even if there is no next wave to create more mages, we have plenty to do for those that are here and they are not going anywhere." He said.

"There was a storm forecast." Aiden piped up. "For all we know that's the wave we've been waiting for. We won't be able to tell until mages start getting powers after it, though, so there's no real use worrying."

Aiden had a way with people, Furcifer had to admit. Probably a relic from his days as a magician.

People even seemed to listen to him. The room quietened down, and Furcifer noticed Ellis and White were making notes and comparing observations between them.

"Now if we can go back to the topic at hand." Furcifer smiled. It seemed they were getting back on track.

Though he had no idea how badly their talks were about to be derailed by events happening only a few miles away.

Chapter 3

It felt like the cat on his chest weighed about ten kilos. The softly purring mass stretched out, yawned, and then continued to pretend he did not exist. The soft paws continued kneading the form underneath him.

Kaoru glanced over at the cat, determined to let it know it had not won. He was still here, he was not going anywhere and he was not giving up on this. The woman under his arm slept soundly and he was not about to betray that trust. Not to mention Jimmy, who had a leg around them both and was currently nuzzled up against his shoulder. He could feel the man's soft lips moving against his skin, and it gave him goosebumps of the best kind. Seeing their tan skin illuminated by the sun, contrasting with his own, was beautiful. The small downy hairs on their arms, the smell of linen. He lived for these moments.

The cat, however, could not care less. It merely glanced at him, then turned, parking its butt squarely near the man's face. Kaoru scowled – he was sure it had just farted at him.

Mina woke up and made a face.

"He does that all the time." She said after a quick wave of her hand to dispel the smell. "Doesn't like it when we bring people home."

Kaoru chuckled. "Good morning." He kissed her forehead, then turned and kissed the cheek of the man next to him.

Jimmy stirred and yawned, his jawline lined with some stubble.

"What time's it?" He slurred, looking around the small room.

Mina grabbed her phone. "Eight."

"Aw man." Jimmy sat up and patted the cat on the head. "I'll go feed him."

Mina smiled. "Thank you, sweetie." She grabbed a robe and got up.

Kaoru slipped out the side of the bed and blew them both a kiss.

"It's been lovely, you two. And I'll definitely text you. But I have to go now." He promised, grinning. This hadn't been the first time he'd spent a night here when he was in town and he was sure it wouldn't be the last.

Jimmy yawned again and held a hand up. There was the sound of dry kibble tumbling into a bowl, and the cat rushed off.

"See ya around, Kao." He said, before looking to Mina. "Want to go again? I can make breakfast and we can have it in bed."

Mina grinned and pulled him close.

Kaoru made a face. The two of them were being so cute! He knew neither of them really expected a text or a call from him but he had truly enjoyed his time with them. They were always open to a night with him at the drop of a hat.

No strings but g-strings, as Jimmy had put it. It had made him laugh so hard after three tequila sunrises. He found his shirt on the floor and put it on.

Jimmy made a face. "You can't wear that again - it's completely dirty." He pulled himself away from Mina briefly.

Kaoru looked down at the stained shirt. A vague memory surfaced of someone walking into him with a hot dog on their way home. The smell of mustard and beer hit him and he threw it into the laundry basket.

"Did I leave any clothes last time?" He wondered, glancing around.

"Here. You're tiny but it should fit you." Jimmy threw him a white shirt with a unicorn on it. The unicorn declared it did not like him, which made him chuckle. The shirt was still about two sizes too big and came to his mid-thigh, but it covered him up fine.

"Thanks!" Kaoru put it on and slipped into his jeans. "I can bring it back."

He doubted the man was in any rush to get it back as there was no way it fit the muscular Jimmy, who had impressed him with his colourful tattoos of horror characters on his arm. He hadn't known who they were, but Jimmy had pointed them out. Frankenstein's monster posed with Vampirella, and bats rose from Dracula's castle behind them. Mina had told him they had met at a horror movie screening, and that Jimmy was getting Mina Westenra added to the sleeve for her.

"Don't bother, it doesn't fit me anymore."

The shutters opened automatically and let in the sunlight to reflect off of the cream white interior of the brand new flat.

"Going to steal your bathroom for a second." By this time, neither of them was bothering to reply – they had retreated under the covers.

He walked into the bathroom and washed his face. Ugh, he was getting stubble. He ran his hand over it then tried to sort out his hair before deciding that was enough for now.

It was time to go. He blew them a kiss and closed the door behind him as he left the flat.

They were such a kind couple! He couldn't wait to hang out with them again. As he put his shoes on he could hear them giggling and moaning.

Right. He had to be at the hospital by nine. Luckily it seemed like it was walking distance from here. He stopped at the cafe a block away from the hospital and grabbed a quick breakfast. It was cold out, but it was that kind of crispness that usually made way for a warmer day.

Life was good, really. His trips to the city were always a fun diversion from work and he looked forward to them every time.

"Morning." He smiled as the server at the bar looked over him. Or more accurately, down to him. People here were so tall!

She smiled at him politely, before handing the man in front of her his coffee and a bag of pastries. "That'll be - hey!" The man grabbed the bag and coffee quite abruptly and started running.

Within seconds, he was gone, and the barista blinked in surprise.

"He didn't pay for any of that!" She said to another barista, shaking her head. "Should we call the police-"

"You know what, I'll get it. Maybe he's just having a bad week." Kaoru shrugged. "Just add it to my total." He knew she'd be expected to pay for that, and that had looked like a large order. It wasn't like he couldn't afford it.

"Well, if you're sure." She said and blinked, surprised. "Ah, so what can I get you?"

"A coffee and one croissant please. How is your week going?" He asked with a smile as she turned around to grab his coffee.

"Going alright except for my dine and dasher. I've never had that happen before." She nodded. "Glad it's almost Friday. Room for milk?"

"Ah, yes please!"

He could see from her eye bags and her wrinkled uniform shirt her night had been as interesting as his. It had been a fun night - there was a bounce in her step and she hummed to herself as she prepared the coffee. The coffee shop was pretty calm - one or two people had come in after him and were admiring the selection of cakes.

"You hear about the hospital thing?" She glanced over

to him and put the coffee on the counter.

He blinked. "Hospital thing?"

"Yeah! I heard from one of the nurses who gets their breakfast here. Apparently there's this guy and he just goes in and he just... heals a bunch of people." She leaned in with a conspiratorial smile.

"You believe that?" He asked.

"I don't know. There's all kinds out there, you know."

A barista appropriate, neutral answer. "What do you really think?" He pushed a little.

"I..." She hesitated then shook her head. "No. I don't believe it. Why would anyone do that without getting paid? And the hospital, they would be telling everyone, right?" She looked up as another customer entered, and the barista came up again.

"I'll get you one of the warm croissants." She smiled and turned around to get a croissant from the oven for him. "There you go! Enjoy!"

He nodded and took the tray. "Thank you." He left enough to pay for the items and a tip, then turned around. The person who had just arrived was studying the menu - a man of about forty, baseball cap on and a bomber jacket who grinned at the barista and called her by name. He grabbed a table by the window and people watched while he ate.

He entered the hospital at nine on the dot, looking around. It had gotten so weird lately. People looked up expectantly then glanced away again. Like they knew him. And there were a lot more people than usual just standing around.

With a brief smile he made his way in, seeing people get out of his way. How nice of them. Maybe they were expecting a celebrity? He made his way down the hall to room 33.

The six beds in the room were taken, he could see from the little window in the door. He reached out to open up the door, when he felt a sudden pain.
How bizarre. Had he pulled a muscle? That usually didn't sound like an explosion. His ears were ringing and he found he couldn't see the door handle anymore. Things were getting blurry. He was falling – into something that felt warm but was very disquieting.
Blood? He looked around and saw the same man from the coffee shop, a gun in his hands.

At least he hoped it was the man from the coffee shop. There was no way that ugly jacket should become the trend for fall – it was horrendous. People were rushing around him, but he could no longer focus. He slipped into darkness.

Chapter 4

"I'm sorry. Did you say... an angel?" Furcifer blinked. He had forgotten all about the whispering that had started when Gabrielle crashed his talk, rushing up to the front to whisper into his ear. He stared at her, incredulously, forgetting about the people around. She had made her way into the room just as he was taking questions, and had come straight up to him to let him know about the shooting. A few people were still awkwardly holding up hands for questions, but even they were starting to catch on something was not right here, and lowered their arms to glance around, wondering if anyone else knew what was going on. Some had started checking phones and chatting to one another.

Gabrielle sighed. "I know how it sounds. But yes." She licked her lips.

"We're keeping this quiet for now. The police contacted your office to get your expertise on it." She glanced around nervously. He followed her gaze.

"See, this is why we can't have nice things." Furcifer said, a little bit amused when she shot him a glare.

This could look bad to the other factions - to see the Elites being favoured in any kind of investigation. There had been whispers about other realms outside of their own. Learning more about this so called angel would increase their knowledge of magic exponentially and potentially open up a whole new world of people to trade with, whether it was spells or magical artefacts. Not to mention how complicated it would get with the magic law enforcement agency in the room.

Furcifer beckoned Aiden over, who excused himself from his chat with ms. Baxter and made his way over.

"What's going on? You guys are drawing attention with all this nervous energy, you know." He said, resisting a peek around to see if anyone overheard their chatting. In these kinds of situations, side barring was not always seen as positive.

"I'm not playing politics right now. An angel has been found." Furcifer said softly.

"Oh." Aiden blinked. "Do you mean like a sighting? Because there have been more and more of those."

Furcifer turned to Gabrielle, loathe to admit he hadn't found out more details yet.

Gabrielle sighed. "No, not a sighting. An angel appeared in a hospital and was shot." She said.

"Shot?" Hissed Aiden, looking over.

"Keep it down." Furcifer said softly.

"He's in the Zeus City hospital, with police officers posted by the door." Gabrielle crossed her arms.

"That's nearly impossible." Aiden shook his head. "I mean, there have been sightings, which have been theorised to be angels using portals to get from one location to the next. If an angel actually appeared here, their portaling magic would be able to cross dimensions."

"He could have been living here locally. He was dressed in pretty human clothes."

"Yeah, while that is an option, he came from somewhere originally." Furcifer rolled his eyes.

That implication was huge - while the existence of angels had been purely hypothetical, and even considered far-fetched by most magic scholars, this would provide proof and access to a whole new spectrum of magic. Maybe even an answer to the question why magic was appearing in this world. However, their faction had taken the initial risk of looking into these angels in the first place. It seemed that had finally paid off.

Furcifer shook his head. "This is big. We cannot keep this to ourselves."
"You think we would have been able to regardless? This wasn't some far off forest sighting with at best a teen with a flashlight and an old phone camera. This was at a hospital and in front of a crowd. There's CCTV footage and online videos of the shooting from every conceivable angle." Gabrielle sighed. "If you guys had a tv here you'd probably have found out before me to be honest."

While the police and authorities were trying to keep a lid on this, it was impossible to impound every phone, every recording device.
"Alright." Furcifer sighed. "We need to investigate this, but it cannot disrupt these talks. That's the last thing we need." He looked around. It had taken them long enough to finally get everyone in one location.
Gabrielle sighed. "I'll take your place." She said. "You go get Twitch, and we'll join you as soon as we can."

"What about..." He nodded his head towards the agents, who seemed to be gearing up to head to another talk, luckily.

Gabrielle pursed her lips. "They'll need to be involved I'm afraid. I'll figure something out." She was much better at any kind of diplomacy than he was.

"What are you still doing here?" She shooed them out.

Manon had grabbed her and Furcifer's bags. "Come on!"

An hour later, Furcifer sat in a cafe across from the convention centre. It was the closest thing to neutral terrain he could find, but it would do for now.

Twitch walked in and sat across from him.
"Hey. I got some info on the angel." He cut to the chase, which Furcifer appreciated.
"Thank goodness. Miss Baxter didn't exactly have much but a promise her faction would help out in exchange for information, when it's information we don't have."
"Lucky for you I have a lot of old books."
Furcifer nodded. Twitch had been a mage in medieval times, who had been brought back by the Witch faction in an attempt to prove magic could bring the dead back. In the end, he had paid a high price for that, and had made sure nobody else could lose as much as he did.
"So what did you find?"
Twitch pulled out a few books, and Furcifer winced at the carelessness with which his friend treated the books. Then again he was the owner of the books and he probably didn't realise their age.

Even so, Furcifer jumped as the book was thumped onto the table.
"Here!" He pointed at a drawing of an angelic figure after some paging.
"They visit earth when they want, sorta kinda. They don't worry too much about dealing with humans as

they can hide their wings using magic... And their magic differs slightly from ours, so it's a drain for them to be here, and it would be a drain for us to go over there. At least, that's the theory that..." He looked for a name then grinned.

"Oh! I wrote that. Wow." He chuckled and looked to Furcifer, who just blinked.

He shook his head slowly. "How old is this book?"

"This is actually one of my newer ones, from 1831. Bought it from a lot found in some farmer's attic. It's very interesting and I've verified a lot of the information in this book. Hopefully I can add the angel chapter to that list." He smiled and looked over.

"And you've just been... writing in it?"

"Well, that's what books are for aren't they? They have information, you add to it." He looked up as Manon came in.

Furcifer sighed. "I can handle a coffee date, Manon."

"Your love life says differently."

Furcifer blinked. "And why would I need such a useless thing as a love life?"

"Anywhoo." Manon got her phone out. "While you've all got your heads buried in books, I got the name of the angel off of a friend who works in the hospital. And I looked him up online. He's on social media!" She grinned.

"What?" Furcifer blinked. That was not something he had expected hearing.

"Yeah, well, he seemed to have managed to get an invite to the new Heartly site. Not jealous. Not jealous at aaaaaall." She sighed.

"What's a heartly?" Twitch piped up. "Also, hi!"

"Hi!" Smiled Manon. "In short, it's a social media place for magic users, but it's new so you have to be invited to use it." She turned the phone so they could see the man's profile.

Furcifer was surprised to see a youngish man with green hair and a genuine smile. Asian features and a few freckles.

"Kaoru Desmond." He read. "Doesn't sound very angelic."

"Doesn't need to. When he's here I'm guessing he pretends to be human." Shrugged Manon. "He's a local to this area, according to his check ins. He's got few friends but there aren't many people on the platform yet so that might be why. He likes Nirvana and is interested in healing magic."

"Well, the Nirvana is a surprise." Furcifer admitted. "Any address?"

"No, but there are frequent check ins at the coffee shop near the hospital, so they might know him there. Oh please oh please let me go start there." She bounced on her chair a little.

"Fine. Go." Furcifer almost fell over as she launched

into a hug.

"What has gotten into you, child." He gasped and pushed her off. "Go hug Twitch or something!"

Twitch grinned and held his arms open for a hug. "Be careful out there." He said.

"I always am. Also I may have had a bit too much of the complimentary coffee at the convention. Mwah!" She blew them a kiss and ran.

"Remind me to order decaf for the next instalment of this thing." Sighed Furcifer. "Anyway. So, where were we?" He started taking some notes.

"Their magic is different." Twitch backtracked. "Let's assume that he is an angelic being and not some kind of impostor, then his magic works differently and it might be dangerous for him to be here."

Furcifer nodded. "How much of a danger is it for him to be here exactly?"

"Not a great deal initially, it seems like he can spend a few days at a time here. But after that there might be consequences."

"Especially if injured." Furcifer sipped his coffee and glanced over. "Can I get you a cup of coffee?"

"No thanks. Trying to cut down." He paged through the book some more.

"The book mentions the angels have been known to have relationships on earth. They're very social so I wouldn't be surprised if he has friends here."

"That could be very useful. I'll have someone look into

whether he has any social media or anything." Furcifer grinned.

"That might be good." Twitch put his book away again. "You are so lucky I live nearby so I could grab the book!" He said, though Furcifer knew he probably had just portalled home real quick, and distance was not that important there.

"The magic community is lucky you're here." Furcifer nodded and finished his coffee. This was going to be a long day. He ordered another one.

Twitch blinked, not sure how he should respond to that.

"Well. Yes. Enjoy your day." He nodded and took off.

His fresh cup of coffee arrived just as Hazel Glover walked in the door, punctual as always.

As her faction kept a close eye on all public displays of magic, he thought she might have been a good start to get information on the angel.

"Nice place." She sat down. "That was a really great talk, by the way, I admire how..."

He sighed. "Yes, I was very good and impressive. But I need to talk to you about the angel sighting." By now the news had spread beyond the one faction, and Manon was scheduling back to back meetings with other faction leaders. He simply did not have time to waste.

"Yes, that was a shame. That happened at such a bad time. Perhaps it was a sign of a magic wave."

"I need to know what you know about this whole angel

thing." He simply said.

"Your faction keeps the closest tabs on this stuff. I'm sure there's some information."

She licked her lips thoughtfully.

"Yes, but it will take me a while. We are not a centralised faction like yours." She said. "I will need some time to gather the info, and then... I want something in return."

Furcifer cocked his head. "And what would that be?"

"We want to be included as an equal partner on the investigation. And for the Elites to back us during the magic conference. We're not exactly..." She shrugged.

"You'll need to give me more than some mad witch's writings for a favour like that." Furcifer got up. He wasn't sure he wanted to risk his faction's credibility over some outdated information.

She put a hand on his shoulder.

"At least consider it. As a gesture of goodwill I'm willing to give some information our last leader kept hidden." She leaned over as she spoke, which gave Furcifer the chills. He did not like people in his personal bubble to begin with, but this?

"What could you have? The recipe for the pumpkin spice latte?"

"Everyone knows that was your faction who invented that crap." She raised an eyebrow. "We deal in the real power."

"Get to the point."

"The name of Hayden Willemeens' killer."

Chapter 5

The sun had set by the time Furcifer returned to the Elite headquarters. The new building was large and modern, and any visitor to the city would think it was some major corporation's head office. Locals, however, were aware the building belonged to the Elites if only because of all the magical fireworks happening around it.

The last few years, magic had continued to make headlines. Gabrielle, and faction representatives like her, had come on the scene to help make sense of what was happening. They would appear on news broadcasts, do press conferences and release statements whenever something happened that had to do with magic.
Needless to say, Furcifer's coarse nature made him less suited for any such role, and Gabrielle would often step in to do the talking while he did the research. And that suited him fine – he had never wanted the spotlight. He was happiest just working on his magic and spells and spell books.

Furcifer jabbed the elevator button then paged through his notes. Gareth Albright was a mage residing on the ninth floor, working on his theories in a nice big corner flat. After his earlier, impressive work for the faction, he had been allowed the funds to chase his dreams of proving not only that there were more dimensions, but to find a way to cross them.

Shaking his head, Furcifer entered the elevator. It slid up until he reached the ninth floor.

As the doors opened he could see the standard kind of hallway for the residential parts of the building. Double glazing, a lovely pot plant here and there, and carpeted floors to dampen the noise and keep things warmer. He barely heard the sound of his own footsteps as he walked up to the door of the mage.

They had spared no expense to make the building both liveable and valid headquarters. Much like the faction, the building had to show with every detail what they stood for - values like hard work, solidarity and excellence. They allowed many to live here for free in exchange for their work, a model which some of the other factions were copying in order to lure blossoming mages who did not care for money, but just wanted time and space to work without worrying about the bills. There was a lovely free restaurant on one of the top floors, providing any member of the faction with free meals. It was a system he had fought hard for, knowing that it would be just how he wanted to live. They paid for it by selling magic books to their own members, universities teaching magic and other factions. There was also the consultancy work which was in high demand - companies approached their faction for advice on magic and magic defence.

Despite his work, the faction was still pushing back against publicly and affordably publishing the books for people outside of the magic community, or those who had not entered it yet. Hopefully he would be able to push that through before he retired. It was hard to think that only a few years ago he had published anonymous spell books, hoping to just get his spells out there to whomever needed them.

He knocked at the door and then tried the doorknob, not at all surprised to find it was unlocked. There was some serious security to get into the building in the first place - not just security guards and badge checks, but also magical spells designed to keep those with false intentions out. Even so, the bag checks and guards did most of the work. The spell work was mostly designed to feel intimidating. Unless someone came barrelling through while loudly thinking about their bad intentions, they were not really strong enough to have any effect.

"Gareth?" He asked, pushing the door open until it hit a stack of books, sending it falling to the floor.

"Be careful!" Gareth reprimanded from the other room before rushing through. "That's – that was ordered in a specific way."

"I can tell." Furcifer said, unconvinced. Still, he crouched down to pick the books up.

Gareth groaned. "Close the door and leave them be! You'll never get the order right!"

Furcifer couldn't help but smile. Since his appointment as leader of the faction he had never been spoken to like this. It was almost... refreshing. And he wondered if this was what people who talked to him felt like.

"I'm Atze Furcifer..." The man started, not sure the reclusive mage knew who he was talking to.

"I know who you are." Gareth closed his cardigan tighter around himself. His brown hair was closely cropped, and he had a single earring near the top of his ear. Around his neck he wore several necklaces, with all kinds of charms, both magical and mundane. The young man glanced over, wanting to know what it was the other wanted. He did not care for pleasantries, obviously.

Furcifer blinked at the interruption, then let out his breath. "I've come to ask you about your progress with the dimension spells."

Gareth almost dropped the cup of coffee he was holding. "No way. I thought higher up couldn't care less."

"We couldn't." Furcifer quipped, before sighing. "I meant. Usually, we would leave you to work on it. That was the arrangement. But... there has been an... event leading to a situation where we could use your... expertise and skill set regarding... dimensions."

"This is starting to sound like a job interview. I'm not sure I like it." Gareth sat down on the table and looked over to the man. "Go on then! What event lead to a situation where my expertise and skill set regarding dimensions would be useful?" There was a bit of mocking in his tone, which made Furcifer chuckle.

"We have a confirmed angel sighting." Furcifer finally said.

"You mean one of them winged bastards flew through some busy city then vanished again? They do that. Last time was a while ago so I figured one would show up." Gareth sounded less than impressed. Furcifer only now realised there was no tv in the lounge – he had probably not heard the news. He chuckled and shook his head.

"The angel is in Zeus City hospital with a shot wound."

Gareth tried to look cool and put his mug down, but it missed the table and clattered to the floor.

"Anyway. That's quite something. I'm guessing the mundanes are all over it?" He cleared his throat and cleared up the mess on the floor with a quick spell. Furcifer guessed it had been a while since any non-magical cleaning had taken place in the small apartment.

"Are you kidding me? The police are trying to keep it under wraps. They're presenting it as an unknown man who had been shot in the hospital by some jilted lover. It is... about forty percent right. He looks pretty human. Very short, green hair."

"Okay. I've looked into the hospital's strange healing events. They all described a short green haired man, who I just assumed would be some rogue mage, not an actual angel. That's quite... something." He repeated, finding himself somewhat lost for words.

"What we need from you, Gareth, is to see if we can contact the angel world. We feel it would be better for the situation to contact them first rather than them finding out about this incident and possibly starting a war on us."

"So you want me to make sure the angels, in a whole different world, don't start a war. No pressure." Gareth chuckled, flashing some small, pearly white teeth in an unconvincing laugh.

"Leave the diplomacy up to the faction. All we need from you is a way to contact them. We don't expect a portal through to the other dimension."

"I'm going to need supplies. I mean, I've got theories." He looked up. "Plenty of them, take your pick."

"Contact Twitch and Aiden. It's all on the faction."

Hey, if they avoided a magic war it was worth a maxed out credit card. Right now he had to go and write some kind of report on this – not just for the police who would want to talk to him about this man, but also for the archives of the faction. not to mention agents Alexis and Ellis.

"One more thing." Furcifer looked over. "I read up on this a bit. The angels have a tome named the Book of Dreams."

"Yes. Their theory is that every dream has or will happen following a scenario in the book. It ascribes meaning to their dreams." He blinked. "Why?"

Furcifer hesitated then shook his head. "No reason." He lied. The book would be very helpful to help him figure out why he was having dreams of war. He needed it. He knew it was a common fault to think the next book, the next tome, would have all the answers he sought but this time it felt real. If Gareth was curious, he didn't show it. The young man was taking the opportunity to not only clean up the fallen mug but to remove a few ceramic bowls crusted with the remains of instant noodles and some bottles of pop.

Leaving Gareth behind, Furcifer walked over to the elevator and took it to the top floor.

Gabrielle was waiting outside of his office. "How'd it go?"

He sighed and looked over. "It's... complicated. Gareth is working on a way to contact the angel kingdom. We kind of want to avoid the angel kingdom having to come find one of their own, injured, without any kind of notification from us."

"But can we be blamed? We have no way to contact them. No angel has made valid, verified contact in hundreds of years. This would just be... harassment, really." She looked over with a sigh.

"I agree." Said Furcifer. "But we need to show them that we're willing to make an effort when it comes to treating one of their own properly." He said.

"So Gareth?" She steered the conversation back.

"He's looking at a way to contact them." He nodded and looked over. "There's not much more we can do yet."

"I guess." She nodded and looked over. "The police are in your office. They want to talk to you about the angel and your findings..." She opened the door for him, more to give him less of a chance to escape than to be polite to him.

Furcifer sighed and looked over to her before putting his hands up.

"Fine, fine!" He walked into the office. At least it was a home game, he guessed. The familiar smells of tea, wine and books appeased him after the unfamiliar smells of Gareth's flat.

His office was bright and well decorated. That wasn't so much his influence as the general work of the interior decorators for this building. They had paid handsomely to get a properly designed building out of it. And there was something to be said about the decor – it was designed to avoid stuff piling up. Plenty of out of sight storage, book shelves and a cleaner who made sure the cups and dishes didn't stack up. However, he had never felt as at home here as in his old rooms, where the mess would just become a part of the decor.

"I hope you haven't been waiting too long, agents." He said as he walked in and walked over to his desk.

"We've been waiting for two hours, mr Furcifer." One of the agents uncrossed his legs, while the other ceased her wandering around the bookshelves to sit down with them.

"I don't actually care. I just said that to be polite." Furcifer sat down at the desk. "You want to know what I think about... the angel?"

"I don't know, is it an angel? Ah, I'm agent Cecil Ellis. This is my partner agent Alexis White." He nodded to the lady who took her seat next to him.

"We've met. I'm Atze Furcifer, head of the Elites, just in case you forgot.. I've not yet been to see your... angel." He sighed.

Detective White ceased his scribbling. "You verified..."

"Yes. Twitch – I mean Asa Ward, who was with me at the time we found out, verified with me that there is a possibility this is a real angel. They exist after all. I've also spoken to other faction leaders who agree that the chances are very high this is the real deal."

"So it's pretty much confirmed." Agent White tapped her foot. "A real angel?"

"It seems so, yes." Furcifer said. "I'm not sure what the implications of that are yet."

"It means they can come through to our world. You would agree with that?"

Furcifer raised an eyebrow at the agent. "I would agree with that, yes."

"But we cannot go to theirs." Agent White stopped tapping her foot. It seemed her nervous tick stopped as soon as she had something to focus on.

"That's... not true. Theoretically we can go to theirs. We just never tried, because there was no proof there was such a thing as the angel world. It was a bit of a crackpot theory. There are some texts out there which mention angels, but often they've been dismissed as hoaxes." Furcifer sighed. It was strange to explain to these outsiders. To them, all kinds of magic were fantastical and almost fictional. It was hard to understand why one would consider and study one kind of magical concept but not the other.

Agent White nodded slowly. "Right. How could there be such a thing, right?" She chuckled and looked over to her coworker, who did not seem to share her amusement. Ellis seemed a lot more professional than White. Furcifer liked him.

"I know how it sounds. But we direct our resources into what we know is true and real." Furcifer said tiredly. "We cannot go hunting for both the Easter bunny and the yeti."

"Of course, of course." Agent White sat up straighter. "But – who decides what is real? I mean..."

Agent Ellis cocked his head. "So these texts, how valid are they? I mean from how you talk about the angel kingdom I'm guessing you haven't had much contact."

"We haven't. "

"Do any of these texts provide a visual representation of this... kind of angel?"

"Yes." Furcifer took his tablet computer out of his desk and brought up the images Twitch had sent him.

Agent Ellis looked over the images. "Some of these look like our boy alright."

"When was this written?" Asked agent Ellis.

"Centuries ago. It's theorised that time in the angel kingdom moves much slower than here, and angels generally have a longer life span. It would make it very dangerous for us to go visit the angel kingdom, even if we could."

"Because spending a day there means missing ages here." Nodded agent White, before she handed the tablet over to her partner.

"It seems this Kaoru fellow gets around if there's writing about him. So is he friendly to us?"

"I would say so." Nodded Furcifer. "Of course, the same might not be said from his kingdom when they find out what has happened."

"I would guess so." She nodded and looked at the text. "So he's been here before."

"Correct."

"It would be safe to say he knows more about us than we know about him." Said Ellis. "That could be a dangerous situation."

"Again." White nodded and looked over. "That would seem to be correct, as mr Furcifer would say. But it also means he knows what kind of people we are already. That should help us."

"Possibly." Nodded Furcifer. "It does seem like the locals around the area know him, so perhaps he has spent a lot of time around there. The hospital has reported these healing events have been taking place for a few years, so there's got to be something we can find on him."

"We put our trust in you." Agent Ellis said drily.

"I'll be writing a preliminary report, and if authorised, visit him in the morning." Right now he would do anything for permission to visit that angel in the hospital.

White nodded and stood up. "Thank you. We await your report." She handed back the tablet with a polite little smile. "And I'll make sure to have you authorised for a visit."

"Could my... fellow mage, Asa Ward, also be authorised?"

"We'll see what we can do." Said agent White.

Furcifer nodded, but despite the agents rising, he remained seated. "Alright. You will have it tonight." He accepted back the tablet and put it away, before walking them to the door. "I trust you can detect your own way out?"

"I trust so." Ellis answered with just a tinge of sarcasm. "Thank you for your time, sir. It's invaluable to us."

Now he really liked him. The mage simply nodded."Goodbye, detectives."

After the doors to the office had closed, Furcifer sighed. This was getting tiring. Working with the police had its merits, but he also had to make sure that he took enough downtime. Once he found a case he really loved, it was hard for him to stop working on it. Gabrielle did help in that aspect – she would let him know to get some sleep. As head of the faction, he had to do more than just research. He represented them all.

He just needed some peace and quiet to write up the report for the police so that they could do... what exactly? He had no idea what would be happening to it after this. They would probably have to set up some sort of liaison office with the other world.

There was a lot to do and little time to do so. He looked around, but for once he wasn't ridiculously eager to start on the work. After a moment he laid out all the notes he had made that afternoon and looked over them. It felt like he was missing something. Maybe, once he had met this angel, it would all make more sense. With a shake of his head, he got up, and left the office.

He didn't think back about the angel case until midnight, when a text on his phone informed him the alarm at his office had gone off.

Chapter 6

Security systems were an actual nightmare for a magic guild. While it was a business's headquarters, it was also a living space for many of the residents. The system had been specifically designed to limit access but also take into account sleepwalkers and other people who needed to use the building after what could be considered business hours. As such, Furcifer's own office and those of a few other high up mages were equipped with a silent alarm, while the main entrances to the building had a guard 24 hours a day.

Furcifer nipped home, though he wasn't sure he would feel safe in his apartment. In all the time he'd been there, there hadn't been a single false positive.

He walked up to the security guard.
"Hey Joe... Did you guys uh... find anything?" He asked, looking over. Somewhere he hoped today would be the system's first false positive.
Joe nodded. "Evening Furcifer... We only saw there was a minor intrusion. Someone got into the elevator and

managed to pick the lock to your office. They weren't caught on camera. It's very likely that they hacked it or... you know, used magic." He made a hand gesture. As a non-mage, Joe had his own way to describe magic. It amused Furcifer every time. Except today. His nerves were shot by the idea his private space had been burgled.

"So they didn't just portal in?" That was a relief to him – it meant they didn't have clear access to the place.

"They didn't... portal in, no. We're still looking through all the footage, but the elevator logs told us someone took the elevator up during a time you were not in. But the lobby gets a lot of foot traffic, and the elevator cameras are being replaced."

Furcifer sighed. "Seems like that camera in the elevator wasn't a bad idea after all....Thanks, Joe."

"Oh! Almost forgot." Joe handed over a key. "Gabrielle said you might want a change of room. She had your most important books placed in a safe in the central hub and she thought you might want to sleep in one of the guest rooms. Fifth floor."

"She's quite right." He nodded and looked over.

The central hub was a marvel of both magic and technology- the centre of the building was just a cylinder, filled with spaces, some lockable. It was a library, a transportation device, a safe, handy storage... On every even floor the central hub was freely accessible in the main hallway, on uneven floors they were integrated into the apartments, and Gabrielle had given him a small apartment on the fifth floor so he could access the hub. She was right to do so- his books were probably safest there. People outside out of the faction didn't know how to operate the central hub, so that meant even if someone got in they would be unable to find the books or notes, or whatever had been left of them.

"Fifth floor. Thanks, Joe." He repeated, peeking at the key. You're a star. Let me know when you've got the cameras sorted!" He walked to the elevator.
He was scared. Not scared. Fearful. His penthouse had always been his fortress - and if it had been one day earlier, he would have been there when it happened. He shuddered and entered the elevator. At least they would have a harder time finding him if they came back for more, and maybe he would use the central hub to store his things in right now. He pressed the button for the fifth floor.
His phone beeped - a message from Gabrielle.

-Asked Joe to text me once you were in safe. Your books are in central hub nook 552, code 9304. Be careful out there.-

Furcifer smiled a little

-Thanks, Gabrielle. I'll be in the room you set up for me.-

-Room? What room?-

He could vaguely see the message appear on his screen before something hit him on the head.
It hit hard, but not hard enough to knock him out. Instinctively, he turned around and kicked, before rushing towards the stairs. There was no security at all on this floor, just cameras, but he knew this building better than his assailants. If he could only outrun them... Despite his dizziness, he muttered a magic spell to keep his wits about him. He bashed open the door to the stairwell and paused a moment, listening for his assailants. Footsteps, hurried, heading his way. More than one pair. With a grunt he grabbed the rails of the stairwell.

It had been a hard knock. He flew down the flights of stairs, struggling to hang on to his consciousness. He held on to the walls, barely maintaining his balance as he ran. He could hear the door to the stairs open, but he was already stumbling through the last door, relieved to see the lounge. Joe was still at his post, and a few mages were talking in the lounge.

"Help!" He called out as soon as he hit the bottom floor. "Someone - someone on the fifth floor..." He said, taking a deep breath and sagging down on the floor. The dizziness was hitting him hard.

"They're right behind me." He took a deep breath.

Joe rushed over and quickly barked orders into his walkie-talkie. There was only a small chance they would catch the attacker - there just wasn't a large security force in the building. Every tenth floor had a security guard, but that was about it. The fifth floor was about as far from security as you could get.

Joe briefly checked his head. "You're going to be fine. Jacob!" He called the other guard over to look after him before rushing to the stairwell.

Furcifer felt like an idiot. He'd almost gotten himself caught off guard.

Joe rushed back.

"They escaped through a portal. We found nothing." He sighed. "I've asked a few of the mages on that floor to look into it."

"Smart." Furcifer had to admit. Portal magic faded easily. Having a mage who was there and could look at it within minutes was preferable over having an experienced mage show up ten minutes later, when most of the magic had faded.

"How are you feeling?" Joe asked, crouching down by him. "What were you doing on the fifth floor anyway?"

"Like I've been hit on the head." He laughed a little.
"Ow. Laughing hurts." He gingerly moved his head to
rest against the wall.

"I should get you a doctor." Joe got his phone out.

"Don't be silly. I'll be fine." Furcifer said. Once he knew
he was safe his body had just... shut down and let him
relax. He felt ok, despite some throbbing pain on the top
of his head.

"And no need to call the police."

"The police? I'm calling Gabrielle." Joe made a cross
sign and pushed the call button.

Furcifer snorted. The woman did reign with an iron fist,
and it was wonderful. She did well, and knew about
everything that was going on in the building. Someone
had to do it - he was not going to spend his time
micromanaging everything when there was studying to
be done. Vaguely he realised Gabrielle probably spent
some time studying as well. He just couldn't imagine
where or when she did it.

Very carefully, he stood up and took a deep breath.
The outside air was helping him regain his composure
a bit. He could hear Gabrielle's voice on Joe's phone,
worried, but also decisive. After a few yes's and nods,
Joe hung up.

"We'll be putting you in a room on the tenth floor,
where there's a security guard. Meanwhile, I need to
look into what happened. I swear Gabrielle mentioned
the books being put into the central hub in the same

conversation where she mentioned putting you up on the fifth floor."

"Shit. Come with me." If the fifth floor ruse had been done by an impersonator, it might as well be that the books were not in the central hub at all. It was a bit of a long shot to verify but he had no other choice. He needed to know his books were safe.

Joe nodded and called the elevator, waiting with him patiently. Furcifer side glanced at him, wondering if he could be trusted. While they slid into the elevator, he got his phone out.

-Joe just called you?-

-Of course he did. I could hear your ego right next to him when he talked. You ok?-

-Just fine.-

He texted back and put the phone away, before looking at Joe again. "Sooo... How's the wife?"

"She's just fine sir. We're still working through that bottle of fertility potion you gave us." Joe replied without missing a beat.

"I hope it helps." Furcifer said.

"Me too." Replied Joe. "It's been a year of uh, vigorous trying." He blushed a little. Furcifer grinned. This big hunk of well-trained man flesh next to him was blushing over the thought of sex. It had to be Joe. Only he was a dork like that.

The elevator finally pinged to the tenth floor, and Furcifer rushed ahead to try the central hub.

The console was built into the wall, across from the elevator. It had doors about the same width as the elevator doors, but only half as tall, and placed about a metre off the floor. The console next to it looked a bit like that of an old fashioned vending machine with its plastic covered buttons with letters and numbers printed on them. Furcifer punched in his identification code, then the number of the safe he wanted to access. After a moment's processing, the console beeped and the screen changed.

"Please enter access code"

Furcifer put in the access code and took a deep breath. Another beep verified that the code was correct, and the cylinder started spinning. It was quite loud, quite a deep sound, and Furcifer loved it. If it had been possible he would have extended the central hub to reach into his office, but the cost of it was just too big when he could just take the stairs down and deposit anything he needed to keep safe. Something his lazy self would have to start doing if he wanted to avoid more situations like this.

Finally, the doors opened, and Furcifer eagerly paged through the works released by the machine.

"It's all there." He breathed a sigh of relief. "I think you may have been influenced, Joe. Whoever was after me had to have come in. A spell that would alter your memories would require touching your skin."

The hairs on Joe's arms had started standing up. "That sounds... weird. I'll check the security cameras. I don't often have to leave the little booth so it should be easy to find."

"Cameras can be erased." He looked over. "Are you ok?" For many non mages, it was frightening to be the unwilling recipient of a magic spell, especially if that spell led to harm. Furcifer had to marvel at the spell – one of the limits of spellwork that one could not directly hurt another with magic. That had been circumvented by merely making him redirect Furcifer to the floor where they had been waiting for him.

"I think I'm fine."

"Good. There's counsellors if you want to talk about it."

Furcifer cut short. He could understand the other was upset, but he did not have the time to go deeper into it.

"Can you please get me a key to a room on this floor? And then... well, take the day off. "

"I don't think that's a good idea, sir." Said Joe. "I'm fine, honest."

"It may only hit you later. I'll call your backup to come in for a few days." Furcifer insisted. In fact they would probably need to up security.

"See it as a chance to do some more vigorous trying with your wife." He said. Even if the man did not go to the counsellor, he would make sure that the counsellor contacted him. This was serious and he needed to be followed up on. Just because he didn't care enough to do so himself, didn't mean he didn't care. He watched the blushing man walk off and sighed.

-I'm taking another room and sending Joe home. It seems someone cast a memory-altering spell on him. I don't like it.- He texted Gabrielle.

He put the phone away and waited for a bit.

This was bad. The tower was not equipped to handle violent attacks - their security was meant to keep out uninvited visitors, and put out the occasional fire started by an inexperienced mage. A fire drill was about the limit to which the guards had been tested.

-Do we need to increase security?- Gabrielle texted him.

He loved that she seemed able to read his mind. In a lot of situations, they were just on the same wavelength.

-Let's talk about it in person tonight.- He replied.

It would be an excuse to have some company, which he really didn't mind with all that was going on. While it was unlikely they would try again today, he did not want to risk it. Aiden would be safe - they would have gone straight there had they known. For now he would not take easy to track routes to get there, instead portalling straight from home. Aiden didn't like it and the house was warded against it, but perhaps he could convince him to drop the wards for just long enough that he could get in and out. If he explained the situation, hopefully the man would understand. He took a deep breath, relieved when Joe's assistant appeared with the key.

"Did he go home? Joe?" Asked Furcifer.

"Yeah." The younger man said, barely stepping out of the elevator to hand him the key.

Furcifer chuckled. "You don't like this building."

"I don't like magic much, sir. I prefer to stay on the ground floor, where the rules of physics still apply."

Furcifer laughed heartily.

"That's a good one." He had to admit. "We all obey the rules of physics. We just temporarily bend them." He took the keys from the man.

"Go back to the world of physics." He did know what the man was talking about - a lot of new mages and non-mages who came up to the tower reported that the ground floor felt much more earthly - they could see people walking on the street through the big glass doors. If you went up to the other floors, you could feel the magic, much like static electricity. It made people uneasy if they weren't used to it. Even inexperienced mages had to get used to it before they felt comfortable with it, and even more experienced people reported not liking the feeling.

The guard took off as soon as he thought it was appropriate. Again, he was alone. With a sigh he checked the number on the key, then walked over to the door. The room was much smaller than his penthouse and every time he consulted his notes he would have to go outside to the central hub, but it was only a slight inconvenience. Right now he would be happy to get some sleep. He stumbled into the room and sighed. It was clean, sparsely furnished, as most people who moved in to the tower brought a lot of their own stuff with them. But there was a nice, warm bed, a somewhat usable kitchen and a bathroom with plenty of towels. And most importantly right now there were no attackers, which he was most happy about. He sighed and locked the door behind him before falling onto the bed. "Ahhhh..." He groaned, barely finding enough energy to kick his shoes off. He drifted off to a dreamless sleep within minutes of falling onto the bed.

Chapter 7

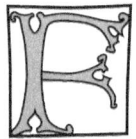

What Furcifer had thought would be a slow, calm day was quickly turning into something completely different as he found himself thrust into this new mystery. Even at ten am he still found himself yawning – he'd gotten up early to write up a haphazard report for the Magic Duo, as he referred to them right now. Sure, he had been keen to show them he was willing to play ball. Didn't mean the report wasn't a steaming pile, with a chaotic amount of information presented as if it was written by a fifth grader on too many energy drinks.

He sent it off via email then called both Aiden and Gabrielle to come meet him.
The facts were... scary. He had been attacked inside of his own fortress, so to speak. His research had almost been compromised and he was feeling almost paranoid, to the point where he didn't know if he could trust Twitch.

Sure, Twitch was currently factionless, but getting this research from him would give him a choice of factions to join. Aiden was the only one who was truly neutral, and even then he had only invited him for a different perspective.

Gabrielle arrived first, her silver hair braided and hanging over a leather jacket. Her biker boots only had a minor heel but even so she had an inch on him. Beneath the jacket, there was a glint of something metallic underneath a transparent top - probably her usual chainmail.
"How are you feeling?" She asked Furcifer.
Furcifer shrugged, hiding a lot of emotions. There was fear, uncertainty, but also excitement and eagerness. If this information, the little information he got in an afternoon, was worth burgling, anything beyond would be bound to be exciting.

Gabrielle shrugged back, kicked off her boots and walked to the kitchen to make herself some tea.
"You want some tea?"
"Just make a pot, Aiden should be here soon as well." He called back.

A brief pause. "Aiden? I thought this would be faction only."

"We need someone who isn't in the faction, Gabrielle."

"Then why not Twitch?" Ah, there was the rub. She preferred Twitch's loyalty to Aiden's independence. Not to mention she had only recently turned his boyfriend into a frog, which hopefully wouldn't come up.

"I don't know who to trust yet." He said honestly. Then again Aiden specialised in electric magic. Disabling the cameras would be easy, and he had once before provided them with invisibility cloaks. His mind tried to come to terms with the fact that he was suspecting one of his oldest friends as Gabrielle came back.

"Maybe you're right." She shrugged. "Did you finish the report for the Magic Law Enforcement Agency?"

"Yeah. They really need to come up with a snappier acronym."

"They do." She agreed and put down a few cups for the tea. "So what did it say?"

"The basics. That we are aware of the possibility of outer-dimensional life that could cross over to our world, but not the other way around. Beyond that..." He opened his hands. "We have a lot of unverified information and I'd rather be holding back than be accused of being wrong."

"What else is new." Gabrielle sighed. "But alright,

you're right. We only have so much information..."

"And I am worried other factions are targeting us." He said with a sigh. "Maybe even Aiden. He has the know-how with electric magic to pull this off."

Gabrielle paused, teapot in her hands, before she poured them both a cup.

"No. I can't believe I'm saying this but we can't get paranoid, especially on mere suspicions. If you're seriously considering him, I'll have someone look into where he was during the break in. But only in the scope of a larger investigation."

Furcifer grabbed a cup of the tea and nodded. "I can live with that." He agreed.

Gabrielle seemed relieved. "So. What have we learned?"

It only took him a few minutes to explain the knowledge he had gathered so far, including Hazel Glover's offer of information. They had requested equal partnership in trade for their information and the name of Hayden Willemeens' killer.

Gabrielle sighed. "I would say no, but that name would mean a lot." She had to admit.

"I think that's why they dangled it in front of us." Furcifer put the cup of tea down and looked over. "I feel like we owe it to Aiden to...."

"We don't owe Aiden anything. The name of her killer doesn't matter now." She interrupted. "I feel bad for him. Really. That was not something that should have happened. But what good will it do now?"

"You're not advocating for revenge?" Furcifer chuckled. "Well, colour me surprised."

"I am genuinely not that kind of person and you should know." With a graceful lean she sat back in her chair, balancing her cup of tea.

"So what's in your report?" She changed the subject.

"Basically what I've just told you. The very basic information I gathered from the books and..." He shrugged. "Whatever I had lying around really."

She nodded. "We need to keep the MLEA on our side, Furce. We've kicked the law in the shins enough for them to be very wary of us." She sighed and swirled the liquid in her tea.

"We were-" He blinked as the chime rang, announcing an arrival. "Ah, must be Aiden." They exchanged a quick look before Furcifer unlocked the elevator so Aiden could come up.

"I think we should tell Aiden what we have right now. Except for the Hazel bit." Said Gabrielle.

Furcifer frowned. "Alright, but only because he will have more information. I could just send the report to Haz-"

"Topic is closed." She raised an eyebrow at him as the elevator showed a carriage was moving up."

Furcifer shut up.

Aiden walked in. "Morning." If he picked up on the mood he didn't show it, but he was always better at deception than any of them. Came with being a show man, Furcifer guessed.

"Hi Aiden, how's Jeffrey?" Gabrielle asked airily.

"Good, he and Oni are great." He smiled a little. "So, what's going on with the angel stuff?"

Furcifer made a face. "We don't have much yet but I sent a report and..."

"And I need to remind him not to make enemies of the Magic Law Enforcement blabla." Gabrielle poured Aiden some tea.

"Did you find any information?"

Aiden nodded. "Some." He leaned over to his bag to take out his notes. "Hate to say it but I think Gabrielle is right there. These guys have the government behind them and they will be eager to show off their authority over us just in case someone else wants to challenge them."

Furcifer sighed. He wasn't wrong, that was the problem. The vibe he got off the agents wasn't exactly the kindest.

"So. We consider them on our side, then?"

"For the time being, yes." Gabrielle sipped her tea.

Chapter 8

Chapter 8 - Furcifer

Furcifer knocked at Twitch's door. He wished he could have taken Aiden on this mission - the man was very down to earth and voiced his opinions easily. Twitch was more introspective, silent. Hard to read. Twitch, however, had the most experience with this kind of historical magical research.

The sandy haired man opened the door, dark circles under his eyes and squinting at the bright light. His pupils were tiny and his usual messy hair was a proper bedhead today.

"Fur -whu?" He asked, looking over. "What time's it?"

Furcifer blinked, astounded. "It's... two pm." He said, checking his watch to make sure he was right.

"Yeah. Sounds about right." Twitch yawned. "I made a sleep spell which backfired. Come on in."

"Thanks." Furcifer made his way into the apartment. As was on par, the man lived on the top floor of the building - like many mages he believed magic was more potent the higher up you got. Furcifer thought it was ridiculous - ever tried muttering a spell on top of mount Everest?

He looked around. Instantly, the smell of magic hit him. Magic had no real smell, but he had come to associate the smell of old paper and the various spices and items and inks used in spells with magic. The flat was old fashioned, with a mixed interior that held things from a standing clock, to an old gramophone player, to a brand new e-reader perched on a reading stand. It made Furcifer chuckle.

"You abandoning the good old paper books?"

"Of course not!" Twitch bristled. "But with time, more and more small mages are publishing their spell books through electronic platforms. And I must admit there are some advantages to being able to put an entire library on a single device." He shrugged a little.

Furcifer nodded. "That's true." He had to admit. "And you've been digitising your own books?" He wondered at the man's progress on that.

"Yeah." Twitch nodded. "That's coming along as well. Scanning and typing." He smiled a little. "Our methods have changed, haven't they?"

"We're still doing the same old things." Furcifer smiled a little. "But there is something I need your help for."

"The big leader of the Elites needs a humble Hopeful?" Twitch mocked.

Furcifer sighed. Sure, he had plenty of mages in his faction. But none had the range of experience Twitch had. Or his wisdom.

Twitch was a special case in the magic community, not in the least because he had been born in the middle ages. He had been burned at the stake as a witch, and in the 1960's, he had been brought back from the dead by seven ambitious mages. The spell had been declared taboo, and Twitch had personally destroyed large parts of it to avoid abuse.

Furcifer took a deep breath and ran him through it again.

"At Zeus City hospital, a man appears every month, healing six of their injured every visit. Strange little green haired man, tiny. This visit he was shot." He said. "He's in the hospital's care right now. Police apprehended the shooter. Apparently he was upset his wife had not been healed by him, and wanted to hurt him for that." He repeated all the facts.

"Human nature never ceases to disappoint." Furcifer could hear some bitterness in Twitch's voice. During their quest for the resurrection spell, Twitch had found inside himself a hatred of mankind, of the people who had burned him, which he had thrust away into a dark corner of his mind to help him accept his new life. From time to time, though, it would appear again.

Furcifer sighed. "Disregard that part. The shooter will get his comeuppance. That part is the justice department's problem. We just need to make sure that the angel, whatever it is, turns out ok."

"How badly injured is he?"

"It wasn't a scratch, but he'll live." Furcifer said. "He was shot. If there is an angel kingdom, this might mean war."

Twitch nodded. "All the information I could find since last time we spoke is… well, unverified." He walked to the bookshelf and summoned a book from the top shelf. It shot down, but Twitch caught it easily, almost nonchalantly. The old paper rustled precariously as he flipped through it, making Furcifer wince.

"Angels are in here… Right next to trolls and fairies." He chuckled. "I guess we'll be able to shift them into the verified section. Most of these are just things I've told you when we met for coffee that day."

"Well, we'll see. I'd like to establish whether he's really an angel – he might just be a healer caught up in some mass hysteria. I'm not believing it until I see wings. Is there anything more you've found since?" He glanced over, really hoping there would be anything that could help.

Twitch continued paging through the book, in a nonchalant manner that made Furcifer wince. He wanted the man to be fast, but he felt like he would scream if one of those pages tore.

"According to this, angels live in a monarchy. One angel is king, or queen, and rules them all from their court. They're only a small group, of less than a thousand beings, consisting of several kinds of angels." Twitch declared, unaware of the mage's internal struggle.

"Of course, I'm reading this all as if it is true. But even if angels are real, their entire society might be very different. Or there could be no society at all."

Furcifer nodded slowly. "You're completely right." He said, looking over. "That book looks old. When was it written?"

"Around my time. People did love to make up stuff back then to keep entertained." He checked the cover briefly.

"You've been on the internet, right? People still make up stuff and pass it off as real." Furcifer shook his head. "Well. Are you interested in going to go see an angel?"

"Yes." Twitch said at once, before running a hand through his hair and noticing his tea- stained shirt. "Just uh, give me a moment to go shower and change."

Chapter 9

Furcifer bounced on his heels, reading and rereading over the questions he had written down to ask this angel when he saw him. His eyes kept flicking to his watch.

He had written out lists of questions, gathered up all his reference works and his writing on the day before. Everything was tucked away in a thick plastic folder which he had stuffed in his messenger bag. Luckily, Twitch had been patient about his excited jotting down of notes from the books they had brought.

Now the hospital would only start admitting visitors by ten am, but that gave them some time to explore. The hospital had been cleaned up after the shooting, but there was a definite atmosphere... Hospitals would never be the cheeriest place, but here it seemed extra sad. As they wandered, he could see some patients glancing at room 33. Strange - it seemed occupied so he didn't walk in, but he consulted his notes. It could be important. Perhaps it was the room where -

Of course. Room 33 was where the angel would heal people, and the room he had been shot at outside. He peeked around, with a degree of morbid interest, for any signs of the shooting, but everything had been sterilised and cleaned. There wasn't even the faintest trace. Twitch ignored it, not as interested in the criminal details of the case.

He shook his head, wondering why the angel had chosen that room. With a frown he noted it down – perhaps he could look at hospital records to see if anyone had been in that room who had been important to the angel. Or maybe the location itself had some specific meaning.

He noted it down on his list of questions and took a deep breath. There were so many questions to be asked... And he just hoped they would get some answers.
"We still have half an hour before we can go in. Breakfast?" Twitch suggested.
"Sure." He had kind of dragged the man here. "My treat. Go find us a spot and I'll get you something."

He ordered two teas, and a muffin for Twitch. The cafeteria was pretty empty this time of morning. The hospital's ground floor was pretty open plan, with a lovely cheery hue of orange and red on the walls. It had a general waiting area, the cafeteria where he was currently waiting and a check-in and information desk, with centrally a large flight of stairs which lead to other, more specialised wards. Furcifer briefly imagined the angel walking in through those big doors, past the coffee area, and into the ward. Which begged the question, how did he get here? He could portal straight into the room if he wanted, but he seemed to appear somewhere outside and then make his way in.

Curiouser and curiouser, Furcifer thought. If he could retrace the man's steps... He got up and looked around. The hospital was built out of sturdy brick, but nothing which couldn't be portaled through. There had to be some other reason. Maybe there was a stop before this one.

He took out his phone and texted Manon.

-Need your research skills. Can you look for any sightings of a short, green haired man near the hospital?-

Her answer came a few minutes later.

-You're going to have to be more specific. Plenty of people running around with green hair dye. Any other clue?-

-Fine. It's the angel thing. You got his social media, let me know what you can find from that.- With that he put the phone away. Not much more he could do right now. Manon was a genius when it came to research, so he just trusted her skills right now. She was the one who had noticed the angel had social media in the first place. Nobody else would have thought to look for any of that.

He walked back to Twitch with the tray and sat down, doling out the order.
It seemed security around the hospital had improved – there were a few police officers patrolling the ground floor.
"Just fifteen more minutes. Yep." Furcifer said, more for himself than anything else. He tapped his foot and sighed, while Twitch was patiently unwrapping the muffin.

By the time ten am came around, Furcifer had had three cups of tea and folded the muffin wrapper into an origami swan. He'd done a pretty good job of it too, considering he'd had to look it up on his smartphone then fold it with caffeine jittery hands. As soon as he noticed visiting hours were starting he shot up so fast he almost tossed the chair back and startled Twitch. He caught it with magic and made it clatter back onto its four feet. Not exactly an elegant entrance, but he could live it down. He cleared his throat and made his way through to the general ward, almost marching to the desk.

Twitch struggled to keep up. "It's a hospital, Furce. Calm down." He said and put a hand on his arm. "He's still going to be there in five minutes."

"Not so sure about that, I have to admit." Furcifer sighed.

The nurse looked up as he entered. "Hi! Talk about an early bird."

"You're telling me." He cleared his throat. "We're here to see Kaoru Des?"

Her face turned. "Let me see if you are on the approved list."

"List?"

"Yes, you should ask detective Ellis or White to add you to it as they are in charge of the investigation, if you haven't been added. Can I get your name, please?"

"Furcifer. Atze Furcifer." He craned his neck to have a peek at her list, which she defensively pulled back. "And this is Twi-"

"Asa Ward." Twitch interrupted.

"I'm afraid you're not on it." She shook her head. "As I said, just contact..."

"You are impeding a criminal investigation by not allowing me entrance."

"That's not what the detectives thought, otherwise they would have added you on the list." She replied, unperturbed. This clearly wasn't her first rodeo with intrepid visitors. "Also, you two don't exactly look like cops."

He threw his head back with a groan, and frantically started searching for the card he had stuffed away somewhere, after letting the detectives leave. He started tapping the number in on his phone.

"Sir. No phone calls in this ward. Please take it outside." The nurse shot him a warning look.

Furcifer stuck his tongue out and stayed in place. "Detective White! How are you this lovely morning? It was great to see... What? Oh yes, I would like to see Kaoru and talk to him but my name hasn't been added, nor that of my..." He smirked at the nurse as it sounded like White was scrambling, before his face fell.

"Tomorrow. Right. Right." He nodded and hung up. "I'll be back." He pointed a finger at the nurse. "Our names will be on that list tomorrow."

"Of course, sir, have a wonderful day." She shot him the most brilliant smile, leaving Furcifer to retreat to his car. Furcifer could hear the sound of Twitch making some apologies then scrambling after him.

"You didn't check... Then again I'm not surprised." Twitch sighed. "We'll see him tomorrow."

"I wrote them a report and everything." Furcifer hated that he sounded a little hurt. "I would have thought..."

"That doesn't matter right now." Twitch said. "They

may not want us to talk to the angel. We'll need to play our cards close to our chest."

Furcifer raised an eyebrow. "I like this new way of thinking from you." Though Twitch was a pack animal, it was rare for him to go against authority. But it seemed he had decided the pack was more important than the authorities.

"Our information is our treasure right now." Said Twitch. "I'd love to see what you guys have so far."

The soft sound of the fabric of his tie sliding against itself was offset by the ding of the elevator. He slipped in and adjusted his shoulder bag, checking his reflection in the mirror. He looked good - a lot better than when he had just gotten back. His hair was cut to a manageable length, he usually found time in the mornings to shave and he was dressed in clothes that actually fit him and looked good on him. It was nice and he couldn't help but feel like it influenced his self-esteem as well. He smirked at his reflection then got out at the ground floor, humming a little tune.

Chapter 10

Aiden had to admit he'd had better weeks.

It had been the anniversary of his wife's death, which coincided with the slightly happier magic convention that was going on. It had been a great opportunity for him - he had been running talks, workshops, and the stall Manon was helping run was taking preorders and selling like a dream. After this convention he expected business to be up. These were long days, and it was tough on him and Jeffrey to run both the shop and this stall, but it would be worth it, he kept telling himself. As he heaved another box of candles up to the table, he stretched out and yawned. Coffee was only a temporary replacement for a full night's sleep, and his muscles ached.

There was also the new case, on which he was merely at the sidelines, an observer looking in. There was a lot of excitement about that, but he had only so much time and effort he could invest in that at this point. Right now he had to put his family and his business before whatever madness Atze Furcifer could drag him into if given half a chance.

But if there was an angel, was there an angel kingdom? His mind reeled with the implications. He knew there was something beyond death. There had to be - only a year ago, during a horrific ritual he and his friends had been forced to perform, he had seen the spirit of Hayden. There had been no question for him now. There was something more out there.

And then there was the rumour from some chatty mages that the Witches did have a name for the woman who had murdered his wife. The idea of him getting that name... It scared him a little, but it would not stop him from using that information if he got it. Every time the tight-knit delegation of witches passed by he wondered, and they avoided him. Perhaps for the best.

He had to admit, with the anniversary of her death, he thought back about that moment a lot. The moment where he had seen her spirit. It had been only a precious few seconds - but he had seen her hazel eyes, the way she looked at him. There was no doubt in his mind it had been Hayden.

"Hey, Aiden." Manon waved a hand. "You doing okay? You seem a bit-"

"I'm okay." He said, glancing over and then crouching down to finish what he'd started. They needed some more of the commuter beads, which were proving very popular with the magical crowd.

"Alright." She dropped it and walked around the stand to check the layout of wares. It was just before lunch so the big crowd of people coming out of talks was due to hit. All in all this had been a great opportunity for the store. And with most mages attending these talks, the store was very quiet, so Jeffrey could run it with shorter opening hours.

"Looks like the solar magic talk ended." Blinked Manon. A dozen of mages were chatting excitedly, and some of them were breaking away from the group to come to their stall. But the main group's attention turned to the muted TV hanging above the stall.

Aiden was glad the thing had been muted. It was bad enough to see people stare over his head as they walked by, but this was something different. Even Manon was looking up.

"Aiden!" She motioned for him to come. "It's about the angel."

"What?" He walked from behind the table and skidded to a stop next to her. With a flick of his hand he raised the volume on the TV.

"-Extra police have been spotted around the hospital, we are not quite sure what is going on but we're hoping for more information soon. There are rumours that this has to do with the alleged angel resting in the hospital, but we cannot confirm that right now, and -" The reporter touched her earbud and looked around.

"The city's new department for magical law enforcement has just arrived on the scene. We hope to bring you more on this story soon."

"Thank you, Cordelia." The newscaster in the studio said. "For now we've been asked to warn people to stay away from the hospital unless they have urgent business, and to keep an eye out for the escaped patient. He is delusional and possibly dangerous, but unarmed." The newscaster read off before an image of the tiny green haired man appeared on the screen.

Aiden blinked. Did their angel escape? He bit his lip and muted the TV again. That could just lead to the worst case scenario, for all of them.

Chapter 11

Kaoru had an advantage he knew the humans did not expect. He actually knew what he was doing.

In fact, it was not the first time he had escaped a hospital, but usually it was far less dramatic than this. A night out, too much to drink, bump your head and leave the hospital via portal the next morning while nobody was looking. Getting records erased was easy enough, if you knew the right people and had money to spend. This time he had been less worried about the trail he was leaving. This whole thing had already gone much too far and he needed to get home to do some damage control. After the last check he had slid out of the bed, taking to the window. This would be painful.

And there was his second advantage. There were angelic agents on earth who would be happy to help him. He had been here long enough to make his stays pleasant and comfortable.

Disadvantages. He was injured and in a lot of pain. To hatch his escape he'd been refusing the painkillers by messing with the IV, so the last twenty four hours had been excruciating and that was before escaping through a second floor window.

The jogging pants and sweater he had requested from a nurse were too big on him, and with the hood on, he saw a comical tiny gangster-like figure reflected every time he walked by a window. It would have been funny if he wasn't trying to keep the pants on him at all times. He tugged up the drawstring on the joggers, tightened them again, and hoped for the best. He had no phone so he was relying on his own knowledge of the city and his surroundings, which was luckily pretty good.

Mentally he listed off the places he could go. There was an office block that had someone, almost like a concierge, on call for him when he was here. With him gone for longer than expected, he guessed the council would have brought someone in to stay on call for him. That was going to be his first point of call.

After three days away from the kingdom, there definitely would be someone waiting there.

He navigated by coffee shops and landmarks, finding the building easily. It had been a while since he needed their help, and it was a shame he had to break that streak now. Taking a deep breath he walked into the building, ignoring the receptionist and walking straight up to the elevator. Annoyed, he eyed the cameras in the elevator. The stairwell had none, but he could not risk making his injuries even worse. The walk here had already hurt a lot and he was looking forward to a portal home and some time in his own bed, possibly with a few ladies and lords of the court. If they promised to be gentle.

Unfortunately, there would be none of that in the cards tonight.

Chapter 12

"You are insane." Sighed Twitch. "He's under police protection."

"They won't let me see him, Twitch. Something is going on." He had called Twitch immediately after contacting the MLAE about the escape. They had been tight lipped and gave nothing away, which bothered him. He was giving away all of his information and they did not share theirs. It seemed... unfair.

There were rumours the angel had been returned. But that was all they were. Rumours. And he'd still been unable to talk to the angel in any shape or form.

"You think so?" Twitch looked over. "Or you suspect so? Because there is a world of difference between those two." The other's voice changed from metallic to life like as he stepped through a portal and walked into the room.

"Ugh! Give me a warning before you do stuff like that!" Said Furcifer into the phone, before blinking and hanging up.

"What? I do not want to conduct this conversation over the phone." He shrugged and hung up his own phone.

"So you just poofed over? This building is supposed to be warded!"

"I know, I wrote the wards." Twitch looked over. "So, we're getting off topic here." He put his phone away in his messenger bag and looked over.

"You said something about plotting an escape?" Twitch raised an eyebrow. "And you know that's stupid right?"

"Stupid it might be, but it's not going to be hard. Hospitals aren't meant to hold people, if anything they want to get you out as fast as possible."

"While that's true, they still have security cameras, a lot of people walking around and some pretty rigorous security of their own. Wouldn't it just be a better idea to get the MLAE to work with you?"

Furcifer sighed. "Okay. We've been there." He ignored the other suggestion. He grabbed a book, looking for a minute before starting to read out a spell, his hand moving over the surface of the table. Immediately it turned into an image of the hospital as he had seen it – the coffee bar and the general admittance area all laid out in place. He pointed at the entrance.

"There was one police officer there, probably more to keep an eye on comings and goings than anything else.

Easy enough to get past to get in, but getting out we'll need some diversion."

"Or use another exit. I don't know why I'm indulging you but go on."

"Right, another exit." Nodded Furcifer, looking over the projected image on the table. "There was one in the back – the emergency room. This would require us navigating through a labyrinth of waiting rooms and care rooms."

"We'd need a proper navigation spell. Easy enough." Shrugged Twitch. "So we get in past the guard and we enter the ward. We were not allowed near Kaoru – what stopped us?" Twitch raised an eyebrow.

"Mostly my manners." Shrugged Furcifer. "There was a nurse with a list of people to let through. If they haven't changed anything, our names will be on that list for tomorrow morning."

"After what happened, I worry they won't let the both of us in." Security would definitely be tighter to avoid hi-jinks such as this.

"But you still have that invisibility spell." Furcifer smirked. "I've used it, Twitch. I know you think it's daft but it works like a miracle."

"So you keep telling me. And I just think it's because you're convinced I'll let you play with it if you butter me up enough."

"Aw, but you gave it to Gabrielle." Furcifer pouted briefly. "It would be useful here. You could sneak in with me."

"So we both end up in the room with the angel. What's the next step?"

Furcifer thought for a moment. "We get him out of there. He can use a teleportation bead or something but I'd need to walk out - the longer I spend in there the more suspicious they'll be of it."

"So far you actually make sense. Please do go on?" Twitch said, nodding his head and staring at the plan on the desk.

"We can make some kind of dummy..."

"No dummies. That stuff only works while one of us is near enough to keep the magic going." Twitch shook his head. "If we had any time we could ask Aiden to craft something for this purpose..."

"No. We don't have time and I don't want to involve him in something that could get him arrested." Furcifer sat down at the desk and leaned back. "On that note, this might get you arrested. Do you want to keep going?"

Twitch sighed. "You ask me now?" He sat down into one of the other seats near the desk. "Sure. Why not. Let's go break an angel out of the hospital. From what you've seen though, is he well enough to move on his own power?"

"Yes, as far as I could tell he was. I mean, he escaped on his own." Furcifer nodded.

"He didn't get far." Shrugged Twitch.

"He will be OK. All he needs to do is drop a bead." Furcifer wiped his hand over the map projection, making it vanish. "How are you getting out?"

"Probably the invisibility spell on the way out, as well. With an extra pair of eyes it's easy to see if we've aroused suspicion. I mean I could teleport with him if he's not strong enough. But I'd prefer to keep magic use to a minimum. Where are we bringing him?"

"We'd be – Huh." He blinked. Whether he took him here or elsewhere could be seen as a political act among the mages.

"Aiden's store. It's neutral ground, though it also means he has to be in on it."

"Fair enough." Sighed Twitch. "He won't like this, you know."

Furcifer sat up and ran a hand through his hair. "He might not. But we're not committing a serious crime. All we're doing is make sure a visitor to our world is not held against his will. That's all."

"Is that what you're telling yourself?" He raised an eyebrow. "Cause I think you just want to get a look at this angel in private."

"What impression does it leave on him, Twitch, to be in that hospital? Sheltered from people. Surely he'll get a better impression of humans when he's among them!"

"You're assuming he hasn't been." Twitch sat up. "He's been here for a while. Manon let me know he's been seen in other hospitals. He's probably seen the worst of humanity. Shot wounds, gun addicts, war veterans, abused families... "

"Then let's show him some good." Furcifer got up. "Be here tomorrow morning, please?"

Though Furcifer knew there was no obligation for the man to do as he said, he hoped he would. He needed his friend right now, perhaps even as much as Twitch had needed him to destroy the spell that had brought him back to life. Finally, Twitch broke the silence.

"Why not." He nodded, walking to the door.

Chapter 13

Furcifer entered, immediately struck by the numbing of the sounds as soon as he crossed the threshold. "Wow." He said.

"You're still not used to the sound numbing, huh?" Aiden looked up from the register. As usual he was dressed casually, but he owned it. This was his turf. Furcifer knew this was where he felt most safe, most like himself. Perhaps he had been retreating into this space a bit too much. But usually, if Furcifer appeared, something out of the ordinary followed. He was counting on it.

"No." Furcifer said. "It's weird to come in here and no longer hear the outside world."

"I've expanded the spell to work the other way around as well. People won't be able to overhear us."

"I must admit that will be... very handy." Furcifer licked his lips and immediately, Aiden knew there would be trouble. He kind of looked forward to it though. He could use something to take his mind off.

"Is this about the whole Angel thing?" He'd followed the angel escape with some interest, but there hadn't been much coverage about it. And to be honest, he had not been particularly interested in becoming more involved with the case considering there was now a magic law enforcement agency. His experience with any kind of law enforcement was... tenuous, at best. There was the matter of his criminal record as a juvenile in the foster system and his time spent in prison before being acquitted of his wife's murder.

"Yes." Furcifer said.
Aiden blinked, waking up from his thoughts. "Mmm?"
"Yes, it has to do with the angel." Furcifer repeated himself. "We're um. Going to break him out of the hospital."
"Bad idea, Furcifer." He shook his head.
"They won't let me talk to him!"
"Why should they? Can you, in all fairness, give me an answer to that that isn't fuelled by your ego?" Oh he knew Furcifer would say it was because he was the best mage out there. The head of the biggest faction. But to non-magical humans, that kind of stuff didn't count for much. To a regular joe, he was just a professional fool.

Furcifer took in a deep breath. "It's information our community needs." He said after a while, and Aiden had to admit that wasn't a bad answer.
"The magic waves have stalled. We still don't know

very much about this power. Perhaps he can give us answers." The redhead continued.

"Or more questions." Aiden stacked some beads on a shelf, Oni toddling after him from behind the counter.

"She's growing fast." Furcifer sounded impressed.

"And she's so smart." He patted the girl on the head, very proud of her. He realised it wasn't just the thought of the law enforcement that made him cautious. There was a little one now, who needed him to read her bedtime stories. Russell was a good father but he couldn't teach her about magic.

"So what do you need from me?" He finally asked.

"Nothing illegal." Furcifer sounded relieved. "We just need a place to stash him. Maybe some records... lost. But nothing big."

"Nothing big huh?"Aiden shook his head. "I'm sure somewhere, somehow I already regret it. What's the plan?"

Chapter 14

Finally, the knock at the door Furcifer had been waiting for. After a quick check - he had a monitor which showed him whoever was in the elevator when it reached his floor - Furcifer let the both of them into his office.

"Hey. You weren't followed?" He asked, a little bit paranoid.

It was only yesterday he had visited Aiden's to get him in on this plan, but so much had happened in the last few days. The attack was still fresh on his mind and he wished he could put it behind him, but every noise still made him jump.

"I portaled." Said Aiden. "Love what you did to the portal reception hall."

Twitch shrugged. "I walked past the agents, waved and then did a circle around the building before going home, commuter beading to Aiden's and then the portal." He said.

Furcifer squinted at him before sighing. "Sounds legit." He nodded after all that. He wasn't sure how well the MLEA could track portals, but it was pretty advanced stuff. Even so, friends meeting up wasn't exactly a crime unless they were caught in the middle of something illegal.

"Alright. Let's get started on this. I'd rather not wait around for them to start suspecting us."

"So we're portalling to the hospital?"   Aiden asked.

"No." Furcifer frowned. "That would draw too much attention. We've got no portalling permissions within the city, so we want to keep portalling to a minimum."

"Oh. Of course." Aiden looked over and shook his head.

Furcifer sighed. "Are you sure you're o-"

"Yes, Furcifer. I'm okay." The utterance was followed by a small smile, as fake as Furcifer had ever seen on his friend. It was the smile he used during performances. And only then when he really wasn't feeling it.

He sighed, not sure if he should bring it up, but if his friend wasn't with it, he could not risk bringing him.

"Aiden. Perhaps you shouldn't go with us on this one."

Aiden frowned at that. "What are you saying?"

Furcifer realised he might have bitten off more than he could chew with this.

"It's just that you don't seem to be at your best right now." He said softly. "Is it because of Hay-"

"I. Am. Fine." Aiden looked over and took in a deep breath. Twitch glanced over as well, but for now was pretending to be more interested in some new books he had added to his study.

"I don't think you are." Said Furcifer, walking over to his friend. It meant they were just out of earshot of Twitch, as well.

"Can you honestly pinky promise me that you're ok?" Furcifer said softer now.

Aiden sighed and looked over. "I dreamt about it. That's all. And all this talk of finding her killer..." He shook his head.

"It's understandable. I can't promise you anything but that I'll be here no matter what you decide to do."

Aiden nodded again and Furcifer found he could not read him. He'd done a lot of growing up from the overgrown teenager he had gotten to know at a funeral.

"Let's get this show on the road. It'll help distract me." He smiled wanly. "And hey. I get to kidnap an angel. This should be fun."

"It's not a kidnapping! It's an aided escape." Furcifer sighed. At that, Aiden did laugh, and it was a relief to see.

Furcifer walked back to the living room, where Twitch had helped himself to some chamomile tea and a book.

"We weren't gone that long." Furcifer raised an eyebrow.

"No, but you're a terrible host." Said Twitch.

Many people assumed walking while invisible was a piece of cake. You could just go wherever and you would never be caught. Furcifer knew from firsthand experience it wasn't that straightforward – you had to make sure not to bump or even brush into people. You could not touch or move anything. Most people noticed those things much easier than one would assume. And you had better not step onto anything that gave way under your feet, like carpets or pillows. Not to mention that any kind of trace could still stick to you, from dirty water from a puddle to cobwebs.

The current environment wasn't too bad – it was easier to walk on tiles than on the uneven pavement where he had first tried it. Hospitals also had large wide doorways and slow moving doors, which was an extra help. Twitch would be fine as long as they stuck together. Confident as always, he walked to the general ward's desk.

"Morning again."

"Hello mr Furcifer." The same nurse as the day before. "Let me check if you are on the list – huh. This is still yesterday's." She paged through the folder but couldn't find the other one. "I'm sorry about that. There must have been a mix up."

"Ugh." Furcifer rolled his eyes. "Of course. They must

not have faxed it through."

"Fax?" The young nurse raised an eyebrow. "Ah, you mean email? I'll check!" She sat down at the desk to check the email account. Furcifer glanced to where he last remembered Twitch being.

He didn't see Twitch move, but there was a moment where the door to the ward stayed open perhaps a second longer than it should have.

"Mmm. We seem to be having some technical difficulties. The email came through but no list attached. I'm sorry, that means I really cannot admit anyone…"

Furcifer took a deep breath. "Well, third time's the charm right? Even when you're not charmed." He winked and paused a moment, listening for the click of a glass bead. When he was sure he had heard it, or something very close to it, he turned on his heels.

"Well. I won't keep you much longer." He said, turning to leave quickly, especially as Ellis and White were coming through the entrance doors.

"Agents!" Just in case that wasn't the click of a commuter bead, he had to keep them out of that room as long as he could. "Wouldn't you know it! I'm still not on the list. Well, I may be. It's just that there was no list sent out this morning."

"Strange." Ellis took out his phone and sent off a quick text. "I'm sure it's just a mix up." He smiled fakely, which Furcifer returned.

"I'm sure." He replied. "So, that means you can't get in, does it?" He grinned a little.

Ellis blinked. "What?" He turned to the nurse, who shook her head.

"Sorry sir. Just for safety reasons, we won't be allowing visitors until we get that list." She said. She was not flinching on that one – she wanted to be sure only the right people went in. And denying someone entry was easier than explaining to her boss what had happened to the precious angel visitor to their world.

"You are obstructing an investigation." White said.

"No ma'am. I'm just following your own instructions. Name not on the list, no entry. No list, no entry for anyone." She shrugged, not impressed by either agent's posturing. Furcifer couldn't help but chuckle as the men hit the same roadblock he did – and at the same time it would keep them from discovering Kaoru was gone.

"Well." Furcifer shrugged. "Nothing for me here then. I do hope you let me know when the list arrives." He could not give up and go too fast or they would suspect he was up to something. It was a hard lesson he'd learned. People who knew him knew what to expect and he seemed to be very transparent.

"One second." White said, and Furcifer tensed up. He closed his eyes briefly and turned to the detectives.

"Was there anything else?" He exaggerated the anything, just to make sure they didn't think he was being too nice about this. He was going for a more... annoyed politeness.

"Yeah. Just need to verify the spelling of your name, so we've got it right for tomorrow's list."

It seemed a feint, but Furcifer indulged her.

"Of course." He started spelling out his full name, trying not to seem too relieved. "No, that's a t, like... tango? I guess. Yep, and then z. Zulu. Not s. Yeah, my name's a real Scrabble winner." He went through the entire thing, getting bored of it by the second f.

Chapter 15

"The angel king." Furcifer sounded incredulously. He had rushed to Aiden's after the scene at the hospital, making sure the agents were not following him. They had seemed too busy with the list mix up to mind him much. It had worked like a charm. Between all the chaos and confusion, who knew how long it would take until anyone found the angel had gone. Luckily, Aiden's flat was beautifully calm as usual.

Aiden was feeding Persephone, sitting on the couch as Twitch and Furcifer spoke. Twitch had rustled up some more information about the so-called angel while waiting for Furcifer to join them. The angel was currently asleep in Aiden's guest bed after a good meal, and Aiden had warned them not to disturb him until he woke up in his own time.

"Yes." Twitch held the book out. It had a wonderfully illustrated text on one page, with a family tree on the other page.

KAORU DES REX

The drawn image of the green haired man loomed over the family tree, the latest descendant of the royal family. He had no ties of marriage yet, and Furcifer wondered whether that was because he looked barely an adolescent or because the book was outdated.
He hoped it was the second.

"So... The angel king gets almost murdered on earth, and I'm guessing he has no line of succession?"
"I'm not sure. This book is from 1800, but even then. If he took the throne in the year this book was published, he might not even have had his coronation ceremony. Angels move very slow, as their life spans are much longer." Twitch summarised the chapter on angels next to the drawing for him. Things were simple enough - it was a very conservative kind of place from what Furcifer could gather.

"But if he got this right, we can assume the author got other things about the angel kingdom right." Furcifer glanced up from the notes.

It could have happened that some people slipped through the cracks into other dimensions, even returning with knowledge. Many had been considered mad men and ostracised from magical circles, accused of fantasising rather than researching. Now it seemed a few of those might receive late credit for their findings.
"So. Is there any way we can reach his... government?"

He wondered.

Twitch shook his head. "I don't know. If he doesn't help us there... maybe Aiden can create a spell to cross these barriers. I mean nobody in recent years has crossed."

"Correction. Nobody has spoken about it in magic circles. Doesn't mean nobody has done it." He looked up. "Even mages have mad scientist types."

Twitch chuckled.

"So you know someone." He concluded.

Furcifer nodded. "We have a young mage at the Elites. We allowed him funds to work on this as long as he finished a project for us first."

"Must have been some project." Blinked Twitch. To give a mage funds to work on what was considered a total folly, their earlier work would have to have been impressive.

"You have no idea. It's like magic velcro." He looked over with a little smirk and then peeked back into the room through the small window. "So we're sure it's him?"

"I would say so, yes." Nodded Twitch, following his gaze. "If it is him, his kingdom will have noticed his disappearance. I expect they'll try and contact us."

Furcifer nodded. "That would save us some trouble." He

agreed, though he worried they would not be friendly. Their king, who had come to do good in their dimension, had been injured gravely. If the angels had not contacted them because they were primitive, this would not help their case at all. If they were not careful, they could even risk war with an entirely new people, who might be powerful beyond all they knew. It was not a reassuring thought.

"It might help our case if we contact them first." Twitch looked up to the other. "What do you think?"
"I think it's worth a shot. I'll contact the faction." He really did not want to reveal the name of the man who had been working on the trans-dimensional spell, for fear of the other going over his head. Unfortunately, it seemed Twitch had noticed.
"You don't trust me?" Twitch raised an eyebrow.
"It's not that. You're not a part of the Elite." Furcifer explained quickly.
"I used to be part of your Hopefuls." Twitch recounted. "Unless someone actually took the time to scrub my name from those records?" There was hurt in his voice as he uttered that possibility, and Furcifer felt a stab in his heart.
"The Hopeful faction doesn't exist anymore, Twitch." He looked over to the other and took a deep breath. He could see Twitch tense up, and for good reason. For a pack animal like Twitch, telling him that the faction was no longer there... You might as well have told him his

family was dead.

"You're still welcome to join the Elite. We'd be happy to have you back."

"No." He said immediately. Furcifer could tell why-things between him and Gabrielle were still tense and there was no hope of that improving any time soon.

"If you change your mind... Ah, want to go for a cup of coffee?" He offered, hoping to lighten the mood. Honestly he thought Twitch could try harder - it had been quite a while since the incident that had caused the breach. And his knowledge would prove to be invaluable.

"Yeah, sure." Twitch conceded. "Let's go. You're buying. And proper coffee shop stuff, not a vending machine."

Furcifer groaned. "Fine." He sighed, getting up. He glanced back towards Aiden. "Want us to bring any coffee back for you?"

Aiden looked up. "Yeah, sure. Soy flat white." He said and then looked back down at Oni grabbing the bottle.

"Sure thing." Furcifer walked out of the sitting area, through the store, and exited the front door. Aiden's shop was such a haven of reliability, of peace, it was almost as dear to him as his own office.

"Coffee shop inside the mall work for you?" Asked Aiden, and luckily, Twitch just nodded. He didn't want to go too far away from the angel's location, just in case he tried another escape, like an idiot. But hopefully, the man and his people would be kind to them. For now he had about an hour to write up a report before he had to meet Gabrielle for dinner.

Chapter 16

By the time they had finished their coffee and returned with Aiden's coffee order, Kaoru had still not woken up. Furcifer had had to leave, to go back to his tower and handle his faction. While it had been fun to get lost in this mystery he still had an entire organisation to run, and he had planned dinner with Gabrielle. Time was running short, but he was good at throwing together reports.

He ran off and to the taxi rank, hailing down an empty cab and squeezing in. Were cars getting smaller these days?

"Where to?"

"Dragon's hoard. Main street." He watched the cab driver lift an eyebrow, then glance over his attire. Sure, he wasn't dressed like the usual fancy client, but he didn't smell or anything. He just shrugged and nestled into the seat, firing up his text editor on his phone. From here, the ride would take half an hour, and that would be plenty to figure out something to send to the agents. Not like he had learned much since the last report they had requested, though he would share some of the knowledge he had learned about the angel kingdom.

"So what'd you put in the report?" It was Gabrielle's first question, coming out as soon as they had done the greeting small talk and sat down at the lacquered table. The restaurant was still quiet, an old fashioned Asian kind of place which he loved. Very expensive, suitable to Gabrielle's taste. He watched her briefly as she unfolded the linen napkin and placed it across her lap.

"What I found out." He shrugged. "Mentioned the sources, that it is Kaoru Des, the angel king. I don't know what they'll do with it now." He glanced at the menu, but he knew what he was getting. A hot pot – and if he was kind enough, the chef would slip in some hot sauce. So far, he had never been kind enough.

"Interesting." She said, leaning back a little. "So no sweeping suggestions and predictions? No theorising?"
"It's a report for the police, Gabrielle. I doubt they'd be interested in my suggestions for angelic diplomacy." He glanced over. "Are you?"
Gabrielle snorted. "Oh, were you serious? I mean, we have politicians and things for that. This is too big a matter for us, sweetie." She sighed and looked over. "There's other people who are more suited. Who are trained to do such things."
He was a bit annoyed at her condescending tone, but there was too much history between them to get angry at her. And to be honest, considering how done he

already was with the conference... There was truth in her words.

"You mean... trained in establishing relations with a people who might be much more sophisticated and not willing to communicate with us?" Furcifer scoffed. "We might as well send Twitch at them. He's at least been around for a while and has all the required reading."

"Don't even start. Twitch might well be asked because he's easier to work with than you are." Gabrielle looked at the menu and then put it down. Her decision, as usual, was made in seconds and would probably be the right one. She was good at that.

Furcifer shook his head and got the waitress' attention to order.

Gabrielle put her order in, for a nice chef's selection of sushi. Furcifer asked for the hot pot.

"I'm sorry, we're out. Can I get you anything else?"

"The - um, beef hot pot?"

"I'm afraid we didn't get any broth in today." She said kindly.

"I'll have what the lady's having, then." Gabrielle looked surprised. "What, something here has to be edible." He said as he handed the menu back to the waitress, who did not seem to take offence to the slight, but gave him a glance of amusement anyway. They were loyal clients, after all, who tipped well.

"How have things been? Outside of the faction."

Gabrielle bit her lip a little. "Things have been okay." She said. "I've been going to the clinic."

Furcifer nodded. She wanted a child. Their relationship had evolved - they had tried to be lovers again, but it had not worked. It had become clear to him that while affection was something he needed, it was hard to get when you were an acerbic workaholic. As for sex, he had no interest to pursue anyone purely for that. While he was no virgin, the itch was just not there. Their relationship attempt had been brief, stilted, and had ended just as quickly as it had started.

She had still tried to have a child, but she didn't want it with him. He could definitely understand her dislike of his genes - he was not social, not very emphatic and very self-centred.

"I'm looking at sperm donation." She cleared her throat. "I'm not getting any younger."

Furcifer nodded. "If you need anything..."

"Yeah, think Twitch would want to donate?" She joked glibly. "It'll be fine. I'm going through all the tests and things." He knew, from the few times the subject had come up, she was worried that she would be infertile or unable to conceive the natural way. But even then there would be plenty of magic spells to help her out with that.

"If you want one of those kinds of babies." He smiled. "With all the magic and powers and stuff."

"I don't know if any baby would be born with magic.

Maybe having a baby with a magic user means it'll
be a lot more likely to have these powers, but I don't
know. I would be happy to have a baby, with or without
magic."
"Persephone was born with magic. Perhaps both her
parents were just active mages." Gabrielle said. It looked
like she had looked into Aiden's adopted daughter, one
of the youngest users of magic in the city.

"What about adoption?" Furcifer said, though he
immediately realised it had been the wrong thing to
say. During long talks she had often told him she just...
wanted the experience of being pregnant. Adoption,
while a good solution, would only make her feel selfish
for wanting that experience.
"Maybe." She said stiffly, not wanting to dismiss it out
of hand.
Furcifer sighed as the waitress arrived with their food.
Perfect timing.
Gabrielle took up her chopsticks gracefully, though it
took Furcifer a few attempts. He took a deep breath and
tried to pick up some of the slippery fish, failing on the
first attempt.

"Ugh." He sighed as the fish slid back down to the
plate.
"Fingers are a valid alternative. It's not considered
rude." Gabrielle said. "Can't believe you're trying new
things." She shook her head.
"I have tried a lot of things." He looked up with a little

grin. "Even Balut when I was in the area."

"Oh now that's gross." She recoiled a bit in horror, putting down the piece of eel she had picked up.

"I was wandering around, starving, and this was the only thing sold by the first street vendor I encountered." He recalled. "I just kinda gulped it in, thinking it was a cooked egg, before I found out what it actually was. I think the vendor was quite amused with me." He laughed.

"I can imagine." She laughed, imagining this ragged looking, bright red haired pale man gulping down an egg. Not to mention his face when he would have realised he had basically inhaled a baby duck.

Furcifer looked over and shook his head. "Go on then. What's the grossest thing you've eaten?"

She shook her head. "I've not travelled like you. The grossest thing was probably that hotdog from the skeezy vendor who had pigeon feathers stuck to him."

He laughed. "I should take you to one of those countries that do whale sushi. I would try that as well. Though seared, maybe."

"It's a date, like you keep saying." She nodded.

"So I'm going to go see the angel again tomorrow morning." He looked up to Gabrielle.

"Did you get permission?"

"I let the agents know, yes." He lied, giving up on the chopsticks and picking up the mackerel with his fingers.

So far she was unaware about the whole escape thing, and he would like to keep it that way. He did not know how far she would go to stay on the right side of the MLAE, especially after their brush with international law in England not too long ago.

"Close enough. What do you think you'll learn from him?"

"Not much. But it's one morning I don't have to go to that law discussion panel."

She shot him an annoyed look. "Don't use this as an excuse to shirk your duties." She warned. "This law thing is as important as the angel discovery. At least make an appearance before zooming off."

"I know, I know." He looked up. "But the angel is much more exciting."

"Obviously. But if the laws come out against us... You're one of the few who are willing to speak up loudly and brashly. The other faction leaders want to be liked., You don't care as much."

"That's an understatement." He poured some soy sauce into the shallow bowl. "I don't really give a shit if they decide to make magic illegal. I'll keep doing it."

"Yes, but others do care. Like Manon."

His head shot up as she mentioned his former student. "She graduated to the Elites, hasn't she?"

"With honours. Her probationary period was exemplary. If you're not careful she could become the next leader."

"It's going to happen someday. I won't be here forever."

Whether he meant because he would retire or because he wanted to travel again, he was not sure. But this was not where he would be in five years. He retried, this time picking up the tiny stack of fish and perfectly seasoned rice between forefinger and thumb. It was pretty good, even though the texture was abhorrent to him.

"True." Gabrielle looked over. She was more concerned with who would succeed her as leader of the Scribes. Generally, people in her faction were less ambitious and eager to take the leadership position. Elite members, however, would happily sell themselves and put themselves forwards for a better position. It would be a lot easier to find a successor for Furcifer than for her. Both factions had the rule that only a member of the faction could serve as a leader, so it was not just a matter of grabbing a member of the Scribes and making them a leader of the Elites. It was just a different way of life and seeing things - they just focussed on their work for the greater good rather than on making their own position better. They just did not value ambition as much.

"You would want her to succeed you?" Wondered Gabrielle. "It's good to know."
"Yeah. She's a good person and I think she's smart enough."
"But does she have the leadership skills?" Wondered Gabrielle, popping a piece of sushi into her mouth with

elegant ease. It seemed to defy gravity between her chopsticks.

"I think so. I mean, she'll have to learn a lot." He said. "But she's good and smart. I like her for it. She's talented."

"Alright." She said, looking over. "I'll make a note of it, cause I know you'll forget."

"Ah, you know me best."

Chapter 17

The next morning it took all of Furcifer's willpower not to go straight to Aiden's. But Aiden had told him the angel would need a few days of rest after two escapes, and that he would probably still be there the day after tomorrow. It seemed the small man had been exhausted, and he didn't want to push his luck. Aiden was right. He probably would still be there.

Furcifer didn't like that "probably", but he did have to admit it would look strange if he suddenly vanished from the magic talks without a good reason. So he showered, dressed nicely, and walked into the convention building. He thought there would be chaos, cancellations, but everything was strangely calm.

Gabrielle looked up when Furcifer entered the main room for the morning keynote talk, which would then become a discussion.

"Huh. No angelic interviews?" She bumped into him.

"I wasn't on the list. Remind me to be nicer to cops." He

whispered back. Another lie. He didn't like this. Sooner or later she would see straight through all of this and he did not look forward to that.

"I will. But you won't listen to me." She shrugged and handed him a copy of the discussion notes they had been talking about.

"I want to add a point to the discussion." He said softly.

"Huh? We've got plenty already." Gabrielle sighed.

"Contact with new dimensions and their people." He simply said.

She blinked slowly. "I think you might be right. With all that's gone on I didn't even consider that..." She said softly.

"Hah, see. Not so useless after all!" This was not so much whispered, leading to an angry hushing from the speaker.

"Is there anything you'd like to add to the conversation?" Ms Baxter asked.

"Yes, ma'am, actually." He got up and smiled as charmingly as he could. "Contact with undiscovered dimensions and the people within. This would be quite... handy for any future contacts."

A murmur went up.

"We haven't even established the existence of other dimensions, yet!" Ms Glover looked up surprised. "Can we please focus our attention on actual issues, which might bring our community down if not treated."

"I... Have some information I cannot make public."

Gabrielle got up. "Please trust us on this. We could have kept this quiet and add it later, but then we might be spending even more time here on amendments and repeals." She said.

"So... Is the angel thing true?" Asked Mary.

"Yes." Furcifer cleared his throat. "This is not to leave this room. I have met the angel and he is a real person, a real angel as far as we can tell. It would be unwise not to use the combined brainpower, and magic power, in this room to think up a solution for this kind of thing. What protocols we need to follow."

There was a chattering among the leaders.

"So this is still secret?" Asked Mary.

"Yes." Furcifer nodded. "We cannot make it public yet, not until the police decides to release the information. It would be irresponsible." He glanced around to make sure he got his point across. The last thing he wanted was some anonymous leak. Luckily, the MLAE had decided to not attend this talk. Otherwise he would not have been able to share this information in any way.

"Of course, of course." Nodded Ms. Baxter. "That's completely understandable. The Canutta coven promises discretion."

Furcifer nodded and looked over to Hazel Glover.

Hazel sighed and threw her hands up. "The coven promises to not talk about this before it is announced to the public."

"And Mary?"

Mary raised an eyebrow. "The Scribes faction is - "

"Mary." Gabrielle sighed. "Just promise."

Mary sighed. "Yes. I promise that the Scribes faction will not publicise anything said about the angel in this room, until the news is released to the public."

"Thank you." Furcifer nodded.

Aiden shrugged. "I represent no faction, but I'll make sure nothing about this leaves this room either." He promised, though he looked quite annoyed at having to do so. He was not exactly representing any interests here - except maybe his daughter's. Which faction she would be able to go to would be highly determined by what he voted on, who he supported here.

"So what's he like?" Ms Baxter asked, looking over.

"I can't tell quite yet. We've only had very fleeting conversations so far." He shot Aiden a nervous glance, but the man just shrugged. He probably should have gone to talk to him, before coming here, but... He had opened this can of worms and he'd have to take care of it.

And from Gabrielle's angry looks in his direction, he knew there would be hell to pay. He had just lied to her about not having spoken to the angel.

Chapter 18

The day drew out as the talks proceeded, though there was a definite change in the atmosphere. The dry air of laws and networking made way for excited chatter about portals and angels, and even just talking to people here and there had been very helpful to Furcifer. He had many notes to go through, and a much better idea of what to ask of the angel.

This time, Furcifer's first course of action was to call the agents as soon as he reached his office. With a sigh he pulled off the tie.

"Agent White." Came through the tinny speaker of his phone.

"Hi! Furcifer here." He grinned. "Just checking you got my report. I asked for it back with gold stars and my office hasn't received it yet."

She sighed. There was a brief pause. "Yes. We've received it, but we have been rather busy. Kaoru escaped the hospital."

"Question. Since he's not really under arrest, is he technically escaping anything?"

"He's leaving against medical advice. How's that?"
There was some acerbity in her voice which Furcifer
really liked.

"Besides, he is a witness in an active investigation and
we cannot just let him walk the street." She continued.
Furcifer guessed that was not true - they just didn't
want the angel to walk among the people until they had
found a way to release the news. That was fair enough,
but then they could not pretend it was for the man's
own benefit. It was more for their own.

"So I guess I can't see him today?" He changed the
subject.

"No!"

   "Twitch! How are you doing?" He asked, grinning
widely. Involving Twitch in this was probably the
smartest move. Twitch knew what it was like to be out
of place - something he and the angel could bond
over.

Twitch sighed. People sighing when they heard it was
him seemed to be becoming a kind of theme these days.
He ignored it.

"Research is going ok." He said. "I've not been found
anything more about Kaoru but he's definitely been
around. I've been talking to Manon. He's been seen in
hospitals around this area for about twenty years. He
always picks just one hospital. His visits also used to be
more random. It is only a recent thing that he picked a
day and a time to visit."

"Mmm. That would suggest a link to the area."

"Indeed." Twitch said. "So I'll keep that up. What else do you need?"

Furcifer paused. "Let's go talk to him. I know it's only been a day, but I feel like we should."

Twitch paused. "Yeah, I'd like that." There was a lot they didn't know, and only so much in the books. "I'll meet you at Aiden's in ten."

Furcifer's turn to pause. "You live way further out than that." He said, before grinning. The man had been two steps ahead of him. "Alright. I'll see you there."

Chapter 19

The mall was just as busy as ever, which made Furcifer relax. The area around the mall had become a bit more upmarket, and so had the stores within. Dollar stores had made way for boutiques, and there was an actual security guard at the entrance these days. The hipsters had remained, but they tended to carry bigger shopping bags than they had done even a few years ago.

Furcifer knew that changed things for Aiden – the rent had gone up for his store. It made the opportunity to get free, faction provided schooling for his daughter even more appealing. It was a tough time, but Aiden's business was doing well. Factions bought from Aiden in bulk and many who had heard about magic and were curious would come by as well. Aiden had discovered many a young mage who had just come into their powers and given them information about factions and their options – another reason the factions wanted to keep the shopkeeper on their side. Faction member or not, the mage was an important figure in their community now. The fact that he had stood up to Furcifer before and had part in destroying the taboo spell that had brought Twitch back from the dead made him even more infamous.

Furcifer walked into the mall, immediately regretting his thick sweater. The inside was heated to insane levels and felt like a sensory overload for the man. There was a sharp smell of lavender from the artisan soap shop, mixing with a cloud of some perfumed clothing boutique with too little light and too many teenagers running in and out. At the same time a busker was playing some kind of mangled pop song cover, but Furcifer threw him some change nevertheless, in the hopes that giving the artist money meant that he would not have to play in a public space like this ever again. He marched towards Aiden's store, barely able to hear his own thoughts. While it hadn't moved since the day it had opened, it seemed to have due to the changes in layout of the mall's floor and the new stores besides it. Aiden shivered as he entered. This could never be replaced by any kind of online shop. The smell of those herbs was just too good. With a little bit of a start, Furcifer realised he could not hear or smell anything from outside as soon as he had crossed the threshold, despite the fact that he hadn't even closed the door behind him.

"You like it?" Aiden glanced up. "The mall was becoming so overbearing I had to tone out down. It's a very localised dampening spell. I updated it to include heat regulation as well."
"Well done." Furcifer nodded, taking a step back and then inside again. The difference was palpable, a relief from the chaos.
"You actually sound impressed." Aiden made a face.
"Ah. You didn't come to talk about my store."

He flipped the open sign to closed, locked the entrance and walked to the back of the store.
"He's conscious and stable. I healed his wound somewhat but it still has a way to go. Twitch is keeping an eye on him as well."
Furcifer nodded. Much as he expected. He followed Aiden into the back of the store. On the arm rest of the couch sat the sandy haired mage, holding an empty cup of tea.

"Hello." Twitch was grinning triumphantly. "I didn't think we could do it. This was... exhilarating." He stood up and poured himself a little more tea, the fragrant green making the place feel even more homely.

Kaoru was lying on the couch. He had changed out of the hospital gown and into a pair of much too large pyjamas, probably Aiden's. The short man seemed to be drowning in the simple cotton pyjamas. Probably very different from the ornate clothes he wore at court.

Finally, Kaoru looked up when Furcifer entered.

"You kidnapped me." He said. "You must really want me to do something for you."

"Not so much." Furcifer shrugged. "Like most of what I do it is merely to satisfy my curiosity. You're a rarity. The first verified angel." He hesitated. "And there is a tome, the Book of..."

"I clearly was not angelic enough." He put a hand on the wound, cutting off Furcifer. "Do humans generally shoot their guests?"

"Only special kinds." Furcifer said. "You are healing people. Why?" For now he could put the thoughts of the tome aside. Hopefully he would find out why the man was avoiding the subject later. There were so many questions to ask and he had to stop himself from going spitfire with them.

"That is your first question? Why I do good?" Kaoru laughed hoarsely. "My, you are special."

"They tell me that a lot." He smirked. "I'm curious about other things, of course. But if you wanted attention there are so many things you could be doing besides healing people. Predict world events. Just float in the sky."

Kaoru shook his head. "I'm not doing it for attention." He simply said. "I just wanted to do a good thing. That's all."

"Ah. Of course." Furcifer was not convinced. But he would find out. The angel started fussing with his nail, cleaning under them with a toothpick.

"So what else do you want to know?" The angel looked at him. Challenging. Daring him to ask. Furcifer squinted a little, but he was interrupted by Aiden.

"What you want for lunch." Aiden said, then turned to Furcifer. "I will not let you exhaust Kaoru. He's still healing."

Furcifer sucked in a breath. "Of course. You are right." He smiled a little. "Yes. Lunch. It's getting late." He got up. "How about I get you guys lunch from the pasta place? It's right nearby."

Aiden nodded. "Sounds great." He agreed. "Get me an Alfredo."

"How is their mac and cheese with ham?" Asked Furcifer, gathering his belongings.

"It's a vegetarian place, Furcifer. They have cauliflower

in theirs."

"Ugh." Furcifer sighed. "Fine. Vegetarian mac and cheese." He looked to the angel. "You should try it as well." He nodded.

Kaoru shrugged. "Sure. I'll give it a try." He did seem hungry - he had been very attentive when the food was mentioned.

"I'll have an alfredo as well." Nodded Twitch, looking tired as he sat back into the couch. It had been a long morning for him, Furcifer guessed. Too bad he would probably only make it longer for him. But he would buy them food to make up for it.

He returned with a stack of boxes half an hour later.

"Lunch rush is killer in this area!" He huffed.

"It's a good place." Aiden shrugged and started unpacking the boxes. "So we have some rules to discuss. I want to make sure you all know - this is my house. If you do something I don't like. You leave." He looked around, eyes lingering on Furcifer.

"Why are you - ugh!" He looked away. Sure, he would probably abuse that if that rule didn't exist but... He felt picked on honestly. "Like I would abuse your - I mean..."

Twitch laughed. "Yeah. You probably would be the first to abuse the rule." He shrugged and looked to Kaoru, who was very carefully opening the box. Furcifer wanted to help him, but he didn't want to patronise the angel either. Finally, triumphantly, the visitor opened the box and dug in.

"Hmmmm... This is a lot better than the hospital food!" He groaned and took another bite.

"Of course." Nodded Furcifer. "This food is meant to be delicious. Hospital food is designed to help you get better." He took a bite of the food himself and sighed. He wanted to ask so many things! And he just realised he had forgotten his list of questions.

"So... You're the angel king?" He started lamely.

"Yep." Kaoru looked up from his food. "Been for almost... huh." He shrugged. "A long time."

"Ah. The question still stands. Why come down here to a world that doesn't know you exist and do good things for them?"

"Because I can." He looked up. "I can heal people. Angels don't need that as much. Humans are more frail and are happy for any help when they are in pain."

"That is true." Aiden agreed. "Our medicine must seem... crude to you."

"On the contrary. We don't have much in the way of medicine. It's been fascinating to see how you use chemicals to cling to life in one way or another." Kaoru said.

Twitch nodded slowly. "I guess that should be taken as a compliment."

"Yes." Said Kaoru with a smile. "It's meant to be."

"So you have no ties to this world. No stake in it. And

yet you do? I don't believe it." Said Furcifer.

Aiden sighed. "Will you leave the man be. He is here is he not? And what kind of tie could he have to this world? He's just doing good."

"I know you can believe that, Aiden. I just cannot." Said Furcifer, leaning back. For now he would drop it, but he would find out one way or another. There was just no way even an angel could be that good, risking life and limb just to do good by strangers.

The rest of the afternoon he spent asking about the angel kingdom. He found out it was a traditional monarchy, with a council of high noble angels advising the king in matters. It was a simple but effective system, with its stability promoted by the fact that angel kings tended to last for centuries. As long as the king had an heir, the kingdom would continue. There had been no major social changes over the last few years, and the population was mostly homogeneous, with only a small population of mixed descent. Furcifer didn't dare imagine what kind of mixes – but he did learn that Kaoru's royal army consisted of these mixed creatures. It gave them a status which benefited them so that they could live their life in peace and not be discriminated against. He told them about the royal families and their blood lines, and told them all about how they married and how they courted one another. Their marriage rituals, their courting rituals, what they had in place for people who wished to divorce. How they settled disputes and how their trades worked. The history of the kingdom and the stories and legends about the first king, the uniter who had rallied the clans to come together, and how those clans became the noble families. Other realms were mentioned, but Furcifer tried to focus on making notes on the angel kingdom only. All throughout, he kept making his notes, writing smaller and smaller to make everything fit.

By the time the sun set, the notes had turned into scribbles as he tried to fit everything he had learned onto the last few pages of the only notebook he had brought. He immediately regretted packing his hoodie light - he did not have enough on him for this encounter.

Aiden just made sure the angel was hydrated and warm, providing water and blankets and making sure the angel did not exhaust himself. Twitch contented himself by simply listening to what the other was saying. He seemed quite intrigued, so Furcifer was doubly surprised he made no notes, as if this was meant to be fleeting, as if they were not meant to retain any of this. Not to him - Furcifer believed this knowledge was theirs by virtue of listening. There was a thrill in finding these things first hand, in being the only one who had this knowledge, present company excepted. When he published this, he would be the first and only one to have written it down. It was a thrill, really. There was nothing quite like it.

Kaoru started nodding off, and Aiden stood up. "Right. He needs rest." He said, throwing a blanket over the angel. "You should head home. It's getting late." He looked over to Twitch. "Want to stay the night?"

Twitch nodded. "Sure! I haven't seen Oni in ages. And Russell makes amazing pad thai."

"You should stay for dinner, he was thinking of making it tonight."

"Hey, you never invite me for sleepovers."

Aiden looked over to Furcifer and sighed. "And you wonder why?" He shook his head. "Go home." He said, walking him to the door.

Furcifer sighed and put the notebook in his pocket. He would be returning to the tower - and it had become a tower of solitude. There were oceans in between him and Aiden, and their relationship would never be as close again. It was a painful thought. He shook his head and walked past the closing stores. The mall was a lot less cheery once it hit seven pm. All the better. His head was so full one loud busker might just have made it explode.

Chapter 20

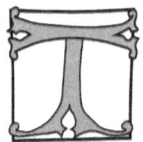

"I feel bad for him." Twitch watched Furcifer walking off.

"Well, don't. He's made his choice." Aiden locked the door again and lowered the blinds on the door to signify he was really closed for the night. "Glad you're back in town though."

"Thanks. It was a nice opportunity." The faction had offered him a temporary job and he had taken it. Lydia, who had been dying to take a break from teaching, had jumped on the opportunity and joined him. She was working an office job and spent most of her free time going to museums, parks, just taking advantage of the opportunity to explore a new country.

After all that had gone on, with the notebooks and her own coming into magic, he was happy she was still there. Her enthusiasm was still a driving force for him.

"So." He cleared his throat. "Yeah, it's a standard one year contract and after that we'll probably head back to the UK."

"Too bad." Aiden walked him into the kitchen. "Oh, is Lydia still job hunting? I've been meaning to hire an extra shop assistant."

"She might be interested, I'll text her." He had to admit. "She's doing office work right now, but I think she would love to do more with magic." He took his phone out and sent a quick text, letting her know he'd be having dinner with Aiden and that he had a job opening she should contact him about if the paper shuffling was getting her down.

"How's she doing?" Aiden poured some water into the kettle and put it on the stove. "Green tea, right?"

"Yep." He nodded.

"You're still avoiding caffeine like I told you?"

"Look, the twitch has only been playing up a little. It's probably nothing. But yeah, I didn't realise how much coffee I was having in the UK." He pulled a chair out.

"Have you seen a doctor?"

Now there was something Twitch wasn't too sure about. "Yes." He lied. "Just waiting for some results."

If Aiden caught the lie he didn't say anything, just turning to the counter to drop some green tea leaves into the pot. Aiden always had the best teas, and he would miss all of this when he went back. There were no convenient magic shops.

"Good." He finally said. "We may not have been able to determine why you have a twitch back in your days or even in the seventies, but right now..."

"How's Oni doing?" Twitch changed the subject.

"Pretty well. She's doing instinctual magic, Twitch. I can't believe it. She's barely walking. Can you imagine what level she'll be at by age five? Age 12 even." He smiled a little, though Twitch could hear concern in his tone.

"I did some research on it." He took out his phone to find his notes. "She might have been born the exact moment a magic wave hit.

"That's impossible. There hasn't been a wave of magic for eight years. At most she's a year old."

"What if there was a small one, that affected nobody else? It would make more sense for a magic wave to taper out from big to small, than to stop all at once." It was a less worrying thought as that meant the magic waves might have returned already, but were just so small there were only a few affected mages. Considering the amount of mages not belonging to a magic community like a faction, it was easy for those to slip through the cracks.

"There is something else I may need your help with."
Aiden said as the kettle started its whistling. "Ah, hang
on." He took it off the stove and poured the water into
the teapot.

Twitch blinked. "What is it?" He was curious now. Aiden
looked hesitant, as if he wished he could take back what
he'd said. Twitch just gave him space, preparing to go to
another subject if the man struggled much longer.

Finally, he spoke up.

"I found out who killed Hayden."

Chapter 21

That utterance had definitely changed the mood in the room, and even more so when he mentioned what he was planning to do with that knowledge.

It had taken him long enough to find the name out when it had been dangled in front of him without anyone actually telling him. That had been the maddening part. But he knew now. And what he wanted to do.

Twitch shook his head as he listened to Aiden. "No. Aiden. You can't do this. It's been..." He shook his head. "She's gone. She wouldn't want you to take revenge for any kind of reason."

"She... deserves to know they won't do it to someone else." Aiden said and looked over. "Is that too much to ask?"

Kaoru glanced over to them both, but Aiden did not want to involve him in this. He had no part in any of this.

"She'll be here tomorrow." He said, walking to the kitchen to start cooking and be away from the angel. "I'm doing this. Twitch. I'm only telling you because... I trust you." He said and looked over. "In case something happens."

"Like what. She tries to kill you for what she's doing? What if she harms Oni, or Russell?" He whispered. "I can't support you in this." He shook his head. "I'll still be your friend. But I can't be an alibi for you on this."

They had parted on serene, if not the best terms. The next morning, Aiden saw Russell off to work, and put down Oni for her nap when the mage entered. The murderer. She had lost the title of mage when she had killed someone.

Aiden flipped the sign of the store to closed and locked the door.
The sound of the lock seemed to spook Violet. She was... taller than he remembered.
"Don't worry. It's just a flip of the latch to get out." He glanced over to her. She stuffed her hands into her pockets. "Violet, right?"
She nodded. "And you're Aiden."

She didn't want to be here, he guessed. Neither did he.
"Tea?" He offered. "I have breakfast tea, earl grey, chamomile..."
"Earl grey is fine." She glanced away. "Nice store. Not as big as the ones we have at the coven, but you know..." She shrugged as her eyes ran over the shelves. It hadn't hit her yet, it seemed. The feeling of familiarity most in her coven had when coming here.

"I know. I provide most of the stock for that store." He looked over. "Just larger quantities. Same selection."

His shop's floor plan was rather small and he would need to start looking out for a larger place. Pretty soon they would need a bigger house for themselves and Oni anyway.

"Ah..." Violet nodded. If she was nervous about this, it didn't show. He had given the coven his word he would not harm her. Either way she looked understandably on edge.

He looked over her. There was nothing. He did not feel hate or anger or fear towards her. All that had happened had happened long ago and if it hadn't been for the birthmark on her cheek he would have been unsure if it had been her.

She'd had longer hair back then, almost to her waist, and she had attempted to hide the birthmark under foundation but it had still been visible. More strange details like those came back. Her dress had been ill-fitting. She had lost a slipper charging at them. The snarl on her face when she grabbed Hayden by the arm when they walked in.

Without a word he walked into the kitchen and expected her to follow.

"I just want to say.... I don't know if sorry is appropriate. I was caught up in a bad crowd and we hadn't set off with the idea of murdering anyone. We just... wanted to scare you. Maybe beat you up so you wouldn't..." She bit her lip. "We reallly-"

"Stop." Aiden said. "You've thought about this. You're sincere. It's all stuff Hazel already told me. She showed me the report that night. You three acted out of your own free will without being directed by the faction. You set off after a few drinks at the bar, came to my show and then forced your way backstage. When we walked into our dressing room, you grabbed Hayden's arm while the other two... spoke to me. Let's call it that. I don't remember much. There was a lot of yelling and then I suddenly got a chair to the head. I went down. Not sure which one of your friends it was but she kept a foot on my head. Hayden...." He bit his lips together trying to gather himself.

She nodded, staring down at her hands. Mercifully, she didn't say anything. This was something he needed to get out there.

"Hayden was-" He shot up so hard his chair fell back. Blinking, he reached down and picked it up, then walked to the counter to make the tea. As the kettle came to a rolling boil he turned around.
"You strangled Hayden. I don't know how the security guard let this happen but I'm assuming you used some sort of spell. I don't remember much after that, besides watching my wife get strangled. Oh, and being arrested after that." He tried to make it sound light, but it was painful. It was heart wrenching to think back about it. At that point in his life it had caused a crease, a before and after.

The silence lasted a little longer. Finally, he put down two mugs of fragrant tea. Violet uncurled her hands and wrapped them around the mug before sipping it carefully.

"This tea is great." She said softly.

"Thank you." He sipped it and then put it down. "Do you remember what happened?"

"I wrote it down in my journal that night. Ever since Hazel told me she'd given you my name, I went back and reread it maybe fifty times. I can't believe I was that person. So much hate and... stupidity." She looked down and drank some more tea, cooling it with a small spell. As she waved her hand over the tea, she seemed to calm down. Magic was what she was confident, comfortable in.

"Sorry doesn't undo anything. But I would give anything to undo it."

"Unfortunately, ever since the Spell was destroyed, there is no way to bring her back. This can't be undone." Aiden said, slightly hoarsely. "She is gone and we are still here."

"Tell me about her."

This surprised Aiden. He wet his lips and nodded.

"I met her when I was auditioning for an assistant. I was 18, fresh out of the foster system, and I had some savings to spend. I bought some illusionist tricks, and put an ad in the newspaper. Maybe three people showed. One had misread the ad and thought I meant a personal assistant. He was mortified, standing there in his nice suit in front of this teenager with garish props." He laughed a little. She chuckled politely and nodded for him to continue.

"And then there was Hayden. Wavy hair that bounced and those big, intelligent eyes. She had this energy, as if she was changing the world with every step she took, but not full of herself. Just... very aware of her potential. I asked her what she was doing here and she said she needed money, and that the 'Hayden and Aiden show' would sound great. I told her it would be 'Aiden and Hayden'. She just smiled and told me, "We'll see.". He laughed at that and wiped a tear.

"We hit it off. I'd never had a best friend but I imagine that's the way it feels, being a teenager with someone you trust that well. Though I hadn't planned on it, I told her about magic, about the spell work. She loved it." He wiped his eyes and got up.

"I need a moment."

"Take your time. Can I pour myself some more tea?"

Aiden nodded. "Pot's on the counter."

"I don't think she had magic." Aiden continued. "But she was happy to know about it, you know? A lot of non-mages who find out these days start wishing they had magic, but she was happy with what she had. Somehow, she knew that what she had was better than magic. We were married six months later." He sat down again.

"It would have been our one year anniversary six days

after the attack. Don't think she had family. Not many people showed at the funeral. Furcifer came. Back then.... I guess still... He was a pain in the ass. For some reason I didn't think anyone else had this power so when he showed up, I thought he was a rival. It annoyed him so much. He just wanted to talk magic and I..." He took a deep breath.

Violet licked her lips and drank some more of the tea. "He is a pain in the ass. Hazel said he wanted me to get all kinds of wards before coming here."

"Did you?" Aiden asked.

She shook her head. "I didn't. I figured I had to trust in you."

Aiden nodded and noted she was half way through her second mug of the tea. He'd handed her the slightly larger one.

"You should probably stop drinking that."

Confusion, then fear, then realisation.

"Hah, you're kidding. I saw you drink from the same pot."

"I didn't poison it if that's what you're worried about. But that anise-like taste in there is Mage's venom." He sipped a little bit more of his own mug. "A few sips will take your powers away for a day or two. I don't mind. I was worried about magically blasting your head off. A mug and a half like that..." He moved his head a little.

Violet shot up. "What have you done to me." She sounded upset more than angry.

He hated that for the last few years he had felt that urge to take revenge, especially knowing Hayden would be the last one to demand a life for a life. So he had not taken a life. He had not done anything he couldn't take back. Still, something remained in his stomach, a feeling he hoped would have lifted.

"I don't think you'll have magic for a few years. Possibly for the rest of your life. I know the two others in the attack have vanished. Maybe they died. Maybe they went into a convent. Who knows. You came here and that took guts, which I appreciate. Maybe I'll even feel bad in a few days and invent you an antidote. But right now I want you to feel what I feel. It's taken years to pick up the pieces of my life, to bounce back from that loss. I'm still not quite there." He looked up.

"But I sure do feel better now." He walked to the door and unlocked it for her.

"Thank you for coming."

Suddenly there was a flash of green as someone came up. Kaoru grabbed the woman's arm and used some energy, taking a deep breath.

The woman pulled loose with a yelp, a flash of magic escaping from her fingertips and hitting the short angel in the face. She ripped open the door and ran.

"What are you doing?" Aiden looked down at the angel.

"You saw that whole thing?"

"Stopping you from a big mistake. Magic is precious. I won't let you take it from anyone for any reason." He pulled himself up and sighed. "She didn't have to magic punch me, though."

"You did kind of come out of nowhere. Did you... undo all of that?" Aiden watched the woman briefly as she ran for the exit, as if chased by a devil.

"Yes." Kaoru sat up. "You're a good man, and I would have stopped you if I had known." He said and took a deep breath. "That took a lot out of me. Magic healing is hard."

"Shit." Aiden sat down by him. "I just... I just... thought I'd feel better. I didn't." He hid his face in his hands.

"Losing a loved one is hard. For your wife, the best thing you can do right now is to live in her honour." Kaoru put a hand on his shoulder. "You scared the shit out of her, though. Maybe that'll make her think twice about her ways."

"She did seem to regret what she'd done. But... she should be in prison. She took a life."

"Life sometimes isn't just. Doesn't mean she's not living with what she did." Kaoru got up. "I'm hungry."

Chapter 22

Aiden had some tea on the counter as he waited for Twitch. Twitch had asked him to please, keep him posted about what happened when he met the woman, and it was easier to tell him in person than over the phone or text. Not that Twitch was super well-versed in using either. And with the magic talks happening not too far away he wanted to keep the store open for people wanting to buy magic supplies.

He took a deep breath and looked at Oni in her cradle, happily babbling and holding her stuffed toy. It was the sweetest sight, and he wouldn't want to disturb it for the world. While at first he'd been distressed about what happened between him and Kaoru, he was calm about it now. Kaoru didn't seem to judge. He hadn't even had to tell him what has happened or why he did it. It was as if he knew already. It made things a lot easier.

In a way, he'd been... embarrassed that the man had seen him do something like this. To be enticed by vengeance. Those were not the kinds of virtues he wanted Oni to inherit from him - he wanted her to be kind, and assertive, but not belligerent.

Twitch made his way in through the store, and into the living area, not minding too much. "Hey. You're okay."

"Yeah." Aiden nodded. "I - Kaoru stopped it." He nodded to the angel asleep on the couch. "But. I took her power. He gave it back to her."

"Aiden! That means... He probably exhausted himself. And she knows you did that to her. Would have done that to her. What if you get the entire freaking coven after you?"

"That's up to them." Aiden poured them both some of the tea, seeing Twitch's hands shake a little. "Have you eaten?"

"Oh. Yes." But Aiden could see the furtive look away.

"You need to remember to eat. It makes the shakes worse." Aiden brought over the mugs of tea.

"I know. I just forget." He admitted and heaped some sugar into the tea. "I've just... This angel thing is... exciting!" He whispered, leaning over the table.

Aiden nodded. He hoped that meant the subject would be dealt with. But no such luck.

Twitch sighed. "I'm glad it didn't happen, for the record. You wouldn't have felt better in any way."
Aiden sighed. He hated that the other was right. There was a good part of him that knew he was right. But letting her get away with it was even worse.

"It's complicated." Aiden said and looked over. "Have some tea. And please. Don't tell Furcifer. I don't want to complicate this even more and I'm meant to be neutral and all that."
"Maybe don't attack people then." Twitch frowned and sipped his tea.
"That's what they should have done." Aiden inclined his head to the side a little.
"Doesn't make what you tried to do any better. It's not like... If it hadn't been for Kaoru. It would have happened."
"Yeah." He shivered. The fact he felt very neutral about this worried him. Or maybe it was just too much to process now, with all that was going on.

Twitch sipped some of the tea and sighed. "Perhaps I'll grab a bite before Kaoru wakes up. Want me to pick you up anything?"
"Oh, sure. Where are you grabbing food from?"
"I'm thinking the pastrami place."
Kaoru shuffled into the kitchen and yawned.
"Meat is bad for you." Kaoru tiptoed to the tap and poured himself some water before looking up.
Aiden still felt weird around the adult angel, who was a

lot shorter than he was. "Are you hungry?"

"Yeah." Kaoru nodded.

"Great. I'll have a pastrami sandwich, and if you can grab Kaoru the vegetarian sandwich. They do a great one." Aiden decided. This would take too long otherwise. "I know Furcifer will probably show up soon anyway."

"Nah. Gabrielle is having him focus on the talks." Said Twitch. "Manon has been running the stand, I'm guessing?"

"Yeah. She and an intern in the faction for extra credit. Don't ask me, she wrangled them into it." Aiden wished this whole angel thing hadn't shaken his whole life up.

Chapter 23

For a change, the convention was going well. It was a less busy day, before the convention's last day tomorrow. Less stressful and important talks and workshops were planned for today with most people just socialising and networking around the many stands. The excitement from the day before had died down a bit as well.

He took a moment to meander towards Aiden's stand, and winked at Manon. "Hey. How's business?"

"Pretty good." She grinned and looked over. "Lots of people stocking up. I may have to call Aiden to bring over more stock." She put another box of commuter beads on the table. "And a lot of people ordered beads to get home after this, so they're picking up their orders today."

"Oh, wow. Makes sense I guess." He said, looking

around. Magic was really changing the world in ways they hadn't even imagined. Not that magical travel was a new concept at all, oh no. Some countries had already implemented laws to regulate magic travel in and around their territory, and almost every big country with a main airport had implemented laws and rules about travelling in via "unconventional ways", as the terminology described it.

Most of the guests were from Zeus City, or not too far out, and were probably just curious about what the deal was with these newfangled beads. While the beads had been around for a while, this was the first time they were available outside of the store. Shipping beads wasn't exactly a thing, due to the possibility of breaking and well, accidentally teleporting some poor postal worker into someone's home.

As soon as those kinks were ironed out, however, Furcifer was sure Aiden would find a way to ship these babies. He ran his fingers over the little glass orbs, each one of them hand-blown by Aiden.

"So how are you? I hear you've been up to no good."
"Me? I wouldn't dare." He glanced around as if looking around to find out who she might be talking about.
Suddenly, a woman pushed past him.

"Put that down this instant, young witch. We will not support this horrible business!" She bristled to a young woman eyeing up a candle.

"Huh?" Was the young lady's eloquent answer. apparently flabbergasted. "It's just Aiden's."

Hazel demonstratively took the bead from her hand and put it back, clearly worried about breaking it. It was almost comical, if it wasn't so unexpected from the meek faction leader.

"Ms Glover. What's going on, please." Asked Manon. "Aiden is a very respected figure in the community."

"You would say that. But I've just heard some news." She glared around. "I've let you all walk over me. Worried what this convention would think about us. But that's done!"

Furcifer blinked, wondering what the hell she was on about.

"I have proof that Aiden attacked one of my mages." She said, and Furcifer felt his stomach sink. He had given Aiden the name of the mage who had attacked his wife.

"You mean the witch that attacked his wife." He immediately clarified, and Hazel's eyes shot fire at him. He had pushed the right button.

"Nobody has been convicted of that. You can't just use that for -"

"True. We in this community, as in yours, like to handle our own issues." Furcifer looked over.

"Stop that. We already know you'll defend your friend no matter what, but he almost took one of my witches' full magical power. The angel saved her!" Hazel cried out, clearly frustrated and upset by Furcifer's rationalisations.

And worst of all, Furcifer had no real idea what she was talking about. He knew it wasn't Aiden's style to hurt people physically and to be honest he had not thought the other would attack anyone. To take someone's power was a big feat, but if anyone could do it, it was Aiden.

But worst of all, the a-word had dropped, and people crowded around her to hear the story. Nobody had had much information about the angel and the news that he was hanging out in Aiden's living room in his pajamas was a bombshell as far anyone was concerned.

To her clear dismay, the onlookers weren't asking about how her young mage was, but wondered about the angel and his appearance. And what powers!

Furcifer sidled away to call Aiden to find out more, or at the very least to tell; him about what had just transpired. Manon was doing a pretty good job managing the shop - people seemed to be more interested in Hazel and her wild story to pay her much mind and she had back up near the table anyway.

He waited for the phone to be answered.

"Aiden! What did you do?" He hissed.

There was a silence, then a sigh. "Did Twitch tell you?"

"Twitch knows?" He sighed. "No, Aiden. Twitch didn't tell me. I want to hear it from your lips."

On the other side of the phone, he could hear the man sighing.

"It's true. I looked up the name you gave me and went after her. I invited her to tea, to talk, and gave her a potion that would take away her magic powers for an unspecified amount of time. Kaoru must have overheard me. He came out and touched her, restoring her powers."

"He did what? He's meant to be resting and not using his magic so he can get back!" Furcifer bustled into an empty room and closed the door behind him.

"What, you think I told him to do it?" Aiden looked around. "I've not asked him to do anything. He just... did it."

"Well, she went to tell her coven and now we've got a nightmare on our hands." Furcifer looked around. "Hazel can be talked down. What's Twitch's view on all of this?"

Furcifer noticed hesitation in the man's voice. "You're... Whose side are you on?"

"The one that has all the magic." Furcifer said. "We can't let this get out. We did more than just get an angel out of the hospital. If the police find out where he is and you..." He frowned as he looked through the glass panels of the meeting room. "Damn. I must go."

"Furcifer? What's going on?" Furcifer almost didn't respond as he tried to make sense of the situation in the main hall.

"The MLAE." He opened up the door. "They're arresting Twitch."

Chapter 24

Furcifer spent the next few days processing his notes. Hours flew by, turning mornings into evenings. If he remembered to eat, it was only because he was reminded by Gabrielle or her forcibly sending up food. Empty plates, discarded tea cups, ridiculous amounts of paper and broken pens. He had to go and get washed up - when he rubbed his chin he felt a clear beard. It made him chuckle. Perhaps he was starting to look like a wizard after all. He stretched out on the afternoon of the third day and grabbed a black bin bag, cleaning up.

There had just been so much to process. Hopefully, Kaoru had been able to rest up, because he hoped to fill in some details he had missed. Twitch had been arrested? He had no idea how or why. And he probably should have asked, but he thought this would be more useful.

His phone, when he found it, was dead. With a grumble he found the charger and plugged it in - there would be some messages, he guessed. He knew the most important things would be coming through Gabrielle but he had heard nothing from her. Which was probably a good sign. And laying low had probably not been a bad plan after breaking the angel out of the hospital. He finished cleaning and threw the trash down the chute just outside his flat. The place immediately looked better, and Furcifer enjoyed not stepping on pizza pegs when he walked around. He checked his calendar on his laptop. It seemed he had missed three meetings, and there was one later today to discuss the angel situation. Well, would he have something to show! He smiled and walked to the shower. It would be perfect timing to show off his findings. He stopped in his tracks when he realised that the faction was not technically involved in the escape. Publishing a book of angel wisdom would basically tell the world that yes, they had done this. It was their responsibility the angel was out in the world. He had to remind himself to contact Lydia - he wasn't sure what Twitch had been arrested for, but he had a creeping suspicion it had to do with Hazel yelling about her mage being attacked. Had she ratted out on Aiden or had she stuck to their unofficial pact to keep this quiet?

"Fuck." He said, shaking his head and stomping to the bathroom. As far as the faction was concerned... He would have to justify three days of sitting in his room, writing, without being able to tell them what it was about. If he made them an accomplice to this angel kidnapping, that would reflect badly on the whole organisation, not just one rogue mage. And even then, as head of the faction they could still believe the organisation was involved.

That was frustrating, to say the least. He shook his head and stepped into the shower. The hot water helped him come out of the trance-like time of studying he had just finished. He took a deep breath and let the water pour over him, slowly letting his mind clear. In all of his studying, one of the most useful things he had had to do was learn how to clear his head. Just... making sure that whatever he was thinking of was not influenced by what he was or had been studying that day. If he did not, he could inadvertently blab about things which were secret, dangerous, or even worse, faction secrets. He had to try and be careful with these things. Try being the operative word here. His brain was a maze of different paths and secrets, each one more ridiculous or dangerous than the last. There was no differentiating until he put it all to paper, and that's why he guarded his notes so carefully. His notebooks were the actual product of his work and he'd almost lost part of that once before. He even had been thinking of hiring an assistant just to digitise his notes – he did not like the idea of writing them down, then typing them in. It seemed a ridiculous amount of work.

He finished his shower and turned on his now halfway charged phone. Many missed messages, of course. And a few voicemails, which he promptly deleted. Who even left voicemails anyway? He towelled off and thought back of his plans to digitise his notes. Manon would do. She had worked with his notes before and knew his way of thinking better than anyone. It would be a wonderful collaboration... And he did kind of miss her. She had been a good friend and he had grown... Well, a bit distant.

He texted Gabrielle. –Is Manon available? I could use her to help manage my notes –

Immediately, she called him.

With a sigh, he answered.

"Where have you been!" She hissed. "It's been three days!"

"I was in my flat, writing. I had a lot to process."

"You did not open when I knocked."

"Of course not. I silence all knocking when I'm writing. You put your phone in do not disturb mode when you're in meetings." He defended. "Is Twitch okay?"

"Yes. They let him go. They thought he had to do with Kaoru's disappearance. They raided Aiden's place."

Furcifer paled. "Shit. Is - Is Aiden okay? Did they take the angel back to the hospital?"

There was a pause, and then the words he had hoped not to hear.

She sighed. "The angels came looking for Kaoru. And guess what, he's gone. And they took Manon as well."

Chapter 25

"They did what?" He felt his blood run cold as he heard that.

"I sent her over to the hospital to find you when I couldn't find you at first, because you said you were going to go talk to him. She was there when the angels came through the portal to collect their king, it seemed. Now both Kaoru and Manon are missing."

He shivered. "Kaoru isn't... Missing." Now he had to come clean. He could not let them think Manon had done anything wrong, and they needed to know everything to get the young woman back.

"What did you do, Furcifer?" Gabrielle's voice lowered, full of rage. "Wait. You- you stashed him with Aiden? Is that why..." She could hear her groan. "You -" A deep breath as she emulated one of the many breathing exercises he'd sat through in days past.

"I ... helped him get out of there." He took a deep breath. "He's safe. I needed to talk to him so I got him out of the hospital."

"Furcifer! For fuck's sake! He was shot! He's not one

of your pet projects! He's a real person, who might be dying without proper medical care! And do you know how it would reflect on us, on us as mages, or us as a faction if we let that happen? Not to mention you did it without a single word of approval from us!" The dam broke as she let that out.

He let her rage on for a bit as he leaned back. Of course, she was right. There was nothing to be said in his defence. He had wanted to know more and he had just taken that as if it was his right rather than actually going about this the right way. He wasn't sure what the right way would have been, probably piss around with the detectives and their inability to tell him what was going on.

"They weren't letting me talk to him, Gabrielle." He simply said at one point where she stopped for breath.

"Then that's their choice! You don't have a right to all that's magical in this world. Until the magic law negotiations finish and we have some representation, we are dependant on what the non-magic people decide. And can I just remind you, you keep blowing off those important talks! And you lied to me."

Furcifer sat up a bit straighter. "They'll happen with or without me. The lying I'm really sorry about."

"I twisted arms to get you in that boardroom!" Gabrielle burst out, before realising. "Sorry. That was mean. I did have to convince them that you were capable. After the museum happenings, a lot of the people in the government didn't want to trust you."

"If we're throwing blame around, Gabrielle, who was it that planted that bangle and started that whole mess?" Furcifer started pacing around.

"I was working for the elites, to get you into their faction." Gabrielle said. "Fine! Whatever. You sort this mess out! I am tired of trying to cover for you."

"As the leader of the Elites, Gabrielle, I'm telling you to back down."

"As the leader of the Scribes, Furcifer, I'm telling you to get your shit together. And find a way to get Manon back!"

And with that she hung up. Furcifer sighed. She had a point. He had had no plan besides getting info out of the boy, and now Manon had been taken by the angel brigade. This was on him. He finished dressing then took the elevator down to Gareth's floor. He would need to speak to the inventive mage, to see if he had already figured out a way to get into the angel kingdom.

As usual, Gareth's room was loud and messy. The door was unlocked, but most people didn't bother going in anyway. He was enough of a loner that he had probably only left the door unlocked for pizza deliveries, from the looks of it. Some kind of loud techno music was playing, and there were papers and take out containers everywhere.

"Gareth." He called out and looked around for the other. Getting no response, he called out a bit louder. "Gareth!" Finally, it sounded loud enough that he could hear himself over the booming music.

Gareth appeared and grinned widely. "Furce! I mean, sir. I mean, Furcifer." He cleared his throat, the enthusiasm remaining.

"Turn that music down, will you? Have you got any news for me? Any progress?"

"Oh! I had to let you know if I made progress?" He blinked, turning the music down. Seeing Furcifer's angry look, he cleared his throat. Still, his enthusiasm hardly wavered.

"I have made some progress. I worked with Aiden and created a teleportation bead that will get you there, and one that will get you back."

"What's the catch?"

"So far... I only have two one trip beads. The production process takes a while and it takes a week to create one, so I hope to have a few more in... a month or two." He cleared his throat. "It'll take a while before we can get a delegation through."

"If we've got two beads we've got two beads." He had to admit his heart sank a bit. Unless Kaoru could return on his own strength, there would be no way to get the bead to Manon and return with her. And he was not sure he wanted to see Kaoru go yet. He had not yet have learned all there was to learn about the man yet.

Gareth nodded and handed over two small pouches.

"The red one is go, the green one is return." He explained. "I'm expecting a new set of these in a week." He said. "And I hope they work, they were a rush order."

Furcifer chuckled. "I'm betting my life on you here Gareth. Give me some confidence."

"Well... Good luck, sir." He said and returned to his paperwork, turning the music up again.

Furcifer sighed at the sound and backed out of the room. Next stop would be Aiden's.

First and foremost, he had to bring back Manon. Manon was more important than anything he could learn from the angel. Not by much, but still. She had not done anything wrong in this and he did not want to see her in trouble because he had done something stupid. Beads in hand, he paced out to the exit.

Chapter 26

Gareth had always been... a character in the faction. He had been proficient in magic from a young age, coming close to what other fields would consider prodigy. His use of magic was very intuitive, but he had studied hard to gain a good insight into how it worked.

At age twelve he had briefly worked at Aiden's magic store, the usual summer job of sorting beads and stacking boxes of candles and teas. From there he had immediately applied to many different factions, with a reluctant but enthusiastic letter of recommendation from Aiden who had witnessed him doing spell work far above his age. He had been approved for the Elite's youth programme, temporarily, but from there on they had found new ways to keep him there. After the youth programme he had gone into the mentoring programme and from there on to the contract projects – a grant of money given to solve a specific magic problem. His first application to create an improved version of cloaking magic had been shot down, but that hadn't deterred him. He had simply returned to the drawing board and had come back later with a grander, better application.

As with most grant applications, he had applied to solve a very difficult problem in magic – permanent changes to the body. Recognising this was something a lot of people were looking for, the Elites had given him a sizeable grant. Where many had failed, he had come out with a comprehensive spell book that allowed changes to the body without the constant need for magic to keep up the effect. The highest echelons of the Elites were still pondering over the leaps and bounds of progress made with this kind of spell work, when he asked for a grant to develop portals to other dimensions.

A smart move from the kid – if his first request had been to work on portals, he never would have gotten the grant. But after dazzling everyone with an impressive spell book, he was given the money without a second thought.

Well, Furcifer had helped him out there. He had promised the young man that if he solved the problem of permanent body changes, he could ask for whatever he wanted next. The young mage had shown a personal interest in the problem of bodily changes, though Furcifer had never asked him why.

Furcifer knocked at Gareth's door and waited. The young mage was usually in his room - he rarely went out. From time to time, Manon would drag him out to some kind of event, but much like Furcifer, Gareth was happy being left alone. Maybe that was why Furcifer liked him so much - they were very similar in that regard. There was little that could distract them from their work, they enjoyed their work and they were happy to do whatever it took to become the best. If anything, Furcifer could see a worthy successor to his position in the boy - but Manon, while not as dedicated, was just as hardworking and much more ambitious. He could very easily see it happen that she got the position purely by applying, while the other did not even take note of the announcement to apply for the job. It was strange to think about his successor... But he needed to think about those things as well.

He knocked again, until the mage opened up the door with a frown.
"You're so insistent!" He huffed. "What is it?"
"Someone broke into my room." He said. "They bypassed the wards I placed on it."

"You locked the door right? I mean wards are good but..."

"Of course the door was locked." He huffed at the younger man. "But I want to know how they bypassed the wards."

"Wards are just like thick spider webs - you can get through it just by pushing hard enough." Gareth said. "You should know better."

Furcifer sighed. It was true. Non mages actually broke through wards easier than mages, who were sensitive to the magic and were very much aware that a ward had been set up. It was more like setting a tripwire than building a wall. If you were running, it'll stop you. If you're walking, you'd get by eventually.

"I will need new wards." He shook his head. "But that's not what I came here for. Did you make any progress with the whole teleportation thing?"

"Come on in." He said. As he made his way in, he saw Gabrielle sitting on the desk, studying some notes. He frowned.

"You got here fast."

"My job." Gabrielle put the notes down. "Should try doing yours from time to time."

Furcifer ignored the slight and looked over to Gareth, who happily started talking about what he had found.

"Aiden's working on the beads, but I've been looking at, you know, portals. Now the problem is someone who hasn't been there can't open one, right?" He looked to Furcifer, who merely nodded in agreement.

"Yes, that would be the big problem... " He said, giving the other the answer just so he would continue on faster.

"And Kaoru is too weak to make a stable portal." He pulled up a whiteboard, which Furcifer didn't like. It meant he would have to listen to something.

"So how portals work is that you imagine the place you're going to. You think about it - you put yourself there, in your mind, and then you do the portal spell. The portal, feeding off of your energy, creates a handy portal to get there. While this portal is open, it saps a percentage of your magical energy, usually between ten and twenty percent per minute. Which means you can feed it for a few minutes, but it will leave you somewhat weakened. Now if you're opening it and step through and close it again in thirty seconds, there is no real issue. You take a breather on the other end and you're fine. But for someone who's injured and who, as you say is using his energy to heal himself, he would be at say, 40 percent of normal energy level." He drew up the numbers on the whiteboard.

"And let's assume that opening a portal to another dimension takes, say, 40 percent per minute. If he opens that portal for even a few seconds, he would be left with critically low energy reserves to tackle anything on the other end. So!" He grinned and capped the pen, making Furcifer sigh. Maybe the lecture was coming to an end.

"What if an able bodied mage managed to feed magic through to him?" Suggested Gareth. "It's the same principle as healing – you transfer magic to heal another. But this time you adapt the spell so that it does not heal, but...refuels the other. That way, you can diminish the effect of a portal to say, twenty percent of power per minute. It still wouldn't be very pleasant, but it creates a stable doorway which everyone can survive. I would definitely recommend he starts resting up to replenish his magic as much as possible, though." Gareth tapped his lips with the pen.

Furcifer nodded. "For him it would be a one way trip, but we'd need to make sure that we can get back home as well. It seemed like it would be dangerous.

"There is no way we can learn a transdimensional spell?" Gabrielle asked, still seated on the desk.

"Ah!" Gareth grinned. "I... don't know. I haven't quite figured out what makes a transdimensional spell different. In theory, once you are over there you should be able to get back on your own power as you know the destination, but I don't know if you want to stake your life on that."

"And after that maneuver, we would have at least one person with us who will be quite exhausted. So we'd need to bring at least three other people. So Kaoru, me, Twitch and..." He looked to Gabrielle.

"You're taking me." She said. "I'm not letting you do something so foolish on your own."

"You can't. The factions would lose two heads." Furcifer argued.

"Yes, but you once told me I have more magical energy than anyone you've ever seen. There is no denying that. I would have won that duel if you had not cheated." She shrugged and looked over.

He grimaced. "That's true. I knew I couldn't last it out with you." He had to admit. "You do - either you use magic very efficiently or your stores are just bigger. But... If you're willing to risk it I'll take you."

"Question is whether I should take you." She looked over. "You're also head of a faction. And as you said no use taking two heads."

"Oh you're not cutting me out of this one." Furcifer shook his head. "I want my notes back, whoever took them, angel or human."

Gabrielle laughed. "Hadn't expected it any other way."

Furcifer nodded. "Glad you understand." He frowned when his phone went off. "Hang on. It's Aiden." He said, before answering.

"Everything ok?" He asked.

"Depends on how you define that these days." Aiden let out a sigh. "Kaoru's son is standing in my store."

Chapter 27

Furcifer arrived at the coffee place a little before twelve. It usually didn't get as much as a lunch rush as the surrounding places as it had stuck faithfully to cakes and scones rather than grilled sandwiches and bagels. He sought out a spot in a corner and sat down, peeking through the menu. It wasn't his kind of place, but he knew Twitch loved it for the coffee-flavoured whipped cream they made. It was all a bit too sweet for him so he stuck with ordering a pot of oolong tea. He couldn't help but think about what Aiden had told him about the man's son. He would have to find the man before he could ask him about all that. For now it helped to focus on the task at hand: to actually find the man.

Twitch walked in, hand in hand with Lydia.
"Hi." Twitch got up. "I didn't expect you to come, to be honest." He held a hand out to Lydia.
Lydia shook his hand. "Finding an angel, how can I refuse? I know, I know. It'll still be a challenge." She nodded as Furcifer shook hands with Twitch.
"True, true." He sighed. "I asked Aiden to send me some

pictures from the security camera in his store."

She turned her nose up. "I don't know how helpful grainy images will be."

"They're pretty good." He got the printouts out of his case. It helped that they had printed them on photo paper, which made them a lot sharper.

"They're not bad." She had to admit, looking over the pictures. "Handsome fella."

"Focus, please." Furcifer sighed. "Also I'm sure he's already like married or something. Are long lived magical creatures your fetish or something?" He sighed, though she just laughed.

Twitch got up. "I'll get us something to drink. Herbal tea?" He offered Lydia, who just nodded.

"Yes please." She smiled and squeezed his hand before focusing back onto the photos before her.

It was wonderful to see her work her magic. Unlike most mages, who learned a variety of magic then focused on their speciality, she had found out she had a talent for scrying before even having had any training. So from the beginning, she had focused on scrying magic, finding spells, location magic, to the point where she was probably the best scryer in the city, if not the country. Needless to say, she was just the woman for the job. Twitch quietly returned with a cup of tea and a coffee with coffee-flavoured whipped cream for himself.

Lydia was already working on a spell, jotting down notes. Scrying was done with a spell first and foremost, but the standard spells didn't always work. Lydia was one of the first who had started modifying all of her scrying spells to fit the target she was looking for, which helped make her one of the most versatile mages.

The scribbling stopped. She sipped her coffee, then started scribbling again. Furcifer, who had been holding his breath, let it out.

"It'll take a while." Twitch said. "Scrying car keys takes about ten minutes. This may take much, much longer." He stirred the whipped cream into his coffee and sipped it.

Furcifer sighed.

"I know. Reasonably I know that. But I'm impatient." He chuckled a little. "So... How have you been?"

"It's been... stressful to move back." Twitch bit his lip.

"Because of what happened?" Furcifer raised his tea cup for another sip.

"No... Mostly because of immigration things. You forget Lydia is British. She's only here on a visa. I managed to get the Scribes to vouch for her, as a visa for work is a lot better way to get anyone over here."

"And I've been their top scryer ever since." She winked, before returning to her hasty jots. "Too bad they don't pay enough for me to only have the one job, though." Most faction work was contracted out, so there was no real steady paycheck from it.

Furcifer wondered how she could even read it, but she didn't seem to have an issue with it. She just continued on making her notes, crossing things out, restarting. It was almost magical to watch.

"I can imagine she's been doing well." He nodded to Twitch, trying not to disturb her concentration even further.

Twitch nodded. "Yeah." He smiled. "She's learning new things every day, so she's happy. And I'm happy when she's happy. And she tells me she's happy when I'm happy." He laughed a little. "It's been nice." He peeked over at her, then smiled.

Furcifer had to shake his head. It was obvious the two adored one another and he loved to see them happy. They were adorable.

"How about another cup of coffee?" Furcifer asked. It had been a bit, waiting for Lydia to finish the spell.

"Nah, I'll switch to tea. Whatever you're having smells good." He saw him glance into the pot and nod.

"Smart plan." Furcifer nodded, getting up to order them some more tea. He walked to the bar and sighed. They were great together. The way Twitch gently moved some hair away from her cheek was just utterly sweet. He'd been like that with Gabrielle, once, long ago. But he was not sure he ever would feel that way about her again after all that had happened. Yes, they were still fast friends and would walk into one another's rooms without knocking, but romance was no longer in the cards. In fact, he wasn't sure when he had last felt attracted to anyone. Maybe it just... didn't happen anymore for him. Maybe it never had. Maybe he had just felt an intellectual attraction to a mage who, at the time, seemed a lot more competent and powerful than he did. Someone like that taking interest in a young man who had just seen his life change - it was enough to sweep anyone off of their feet.

Or maybe the old adage rang true - he just had to wait for the one, whatever or whoever that was. He ordered a large pot of oolong tea, paid, and carried it back to the table.

In the meantime, a waitress had removed their empty cups - and seemingly provided them with more napkins. Lydia had run out of paper, and had started writing on napkins she found on the table. Furcifer poured her and Twitch some tea from the big pot.

Lydia looked up, drank some of the tea, made a face. "That's not the coffee I ordered."

Twitch chuckled. "It had gone cold so I finished it and Furcifer poured you some fresh tea. It's...?" He looked to Furcifer.

"Oh! Oolong tea."

"Eh." She sipped it again, then restarted the scribbles. "Almost done. They are in the city, right?"

"Most likely." Furcifer said. "It didn't seem like Kaoru had enough energy to teleport anywhere."

Lydia nodded. "I hope so. The spell to find someone not

in this city would take a lot longer. I'm almost done though, keep your shirt on."

Furcifer sat up indignantly. "I didn't rush you." He protested.

"You were thinking of it. I've been working at it for 45 minutes now. And even I'm getting impatient to use this." She stretched out. "Let's do this." She grinned and looked over.

"We'll need to head outside. The closer we can come to the centre of the city, the better."

"Isn't there a statue in the middle of the city? We can start there." Furcifer proposed.

"Sounds perfect." She nodded and sipped her tea. "How about we finish this tea then go? We still have plenty of hours of daylight left."

"Luckily, yeah." Nodded Twitch, sipping some of the tea. "You actually like this?" He wondered.

Furcifer sighed. "I bought it for you guys. You don't get to complain."

"I'm just saying. It smelled better than it tastes."

"It's called life. Get over it." Furcifer replied acridly.

Chapter 28

They got to the city centre at just around five. The statue was a bit of an oasis in the middle of the crowded area - there was a train station just across from it. The mass of commuters just streamed by them, walking into the station, out of it, past it.

Lydia took in a deep breath. "Can we actually do magic with all these people around?"
"If we want it to be quiet here... We'd have to rent the area as if we're doing a film shoot. Done it before." Furcifer shrugged. "Just prohibitively expensive. Not something we do often. But we've got to be fast today, so it's not an option."
Twitch nodded. "The Elites must be rich."
"We're selling books now. And teaching classes at universities. We've developed quite a few new revenue streams." He shrugged.
"Of course." Twitch sounded unimpressed.
"Shhh." Lydia put a finger to their lips. "Either say the spell with me or shut up!"
Furcifer squinted at the paper in her hand - there was

no way he could read that. He shook his head and made a zipping gesture over his mouth.

Twitch nodded and did the same. It seemed he didn't want to mess up the spell - Furcifer had seen him mouth some of the first words on the page before stopping.

"Good." Lydia took a deep breath and started her chant. It was light, airy but complicated.

Furcifer had learned that the way one wrote spells told a lot about their personality. Young people tended to forego formality for simplicity, while some, no matter what age, preferred archaic terms and tones. That was the beauty of magic - it didn't matter how you did it or why. It just worked, as long as you obeyed to the basic laws. Sometimes it felt like magic had a mind of its own, and Furcifer thought he would never be able to figure it out. It was a wondrous field to study.

People walked around them in a huge arch - while magic in the street was becoming more and more common, many people who did not practice magic could not tell the difference between a spell to summon cute stuffed teddy bears or an apocalypse of zombies. So they tended to keep their distance, not even filming or photographing them. Not that there was much to see - a thirty something redhead, a twitchy sandy haired man and a young woman with a British accent reciting a long spell.

It was about fifteen minutes before she finished.
"Phew!" She sighed, before looking up again. "I've got a trail." She whispered, starting to walk towards the main street. Twitch and Furcifer scrambled to keep up. Once a scryer got a trail, it was best to keep up with them. They would move fast to avoid losing the trail, as there was no way, short of reciting the whole spell again, to find the trail again. And with a spell that lasted fifteen minutes just to recite, that was a risk nobody wanted to take. So they hurried as best as they could to keep up with the woman, who seemed to be drawn along by an invisible force. Every step she took was self-assured and fast.

Furcifer suddenly did figure out why Twitch was in such good shape. He probably had done scry hunts like this many times before, each of them at the high pace the woman kept up effortlessly.
They swerved through streets, alleys, making sharp, unexpected turns and then following long roads for miles on end. Lydia's pace never slowed. Furcifer, who considered himself to be minimally in shape, had a hard time keeping up with her. After an hour, they stopped at a small house, near the edge of the city.

"Here. It's unlocked. He doesn't fear us." Lydia said, before stretching out. "I want a hot chocolate."

Twitch pulled her close into a hug. "We'll go for one soon. You want to wait outside?" He asked, seeing her energy levels drop.

"Hell no. I want to see the angel!" She huffed. Twitch shrugged at Furcifer.

"Fine! We'll all go." He sighed, opening the door. Very little, however, could have prepared him for what he found.

Chapter 29

In the middle of the lounge, on the shag rug, Kaoru lay naked, with Agnes and Manon. Their chests were heaving, hair sticking to their sweaty faces.

"Oh! Oh god." Furcifer looked away, but not before catching an eyeful of green pubic hairs. "Cov - Cover yourselves up!"

"Fine." Agnes shrugged, pulling the blanket off of the couch and over them.

"And Manon! You got back!" Furcifer called out, surprised. "Are you okay?"

Manon laughed. "Yeah. I'm fine, no worries." She said. "I - kept trying to create a portal home. Kaoru tried as well, and our portals must have connected to one another or something, because suddenly I could just-step through."

"A portal connection?" Furcifer shook his head. The concept was hotly debated- it was theorised that if one person at point A tried to make a portal to point B at the same time as a person at point B tried to make a portal to point A, it would link the portals and increase their strength. As portals themselves were still being studied, nobody had set up an experiment to try out the theory yet.

It was possible, at the very least.

"Well. I'm glad you're safe..." Furcifer sighed and sat down by her to look her over.

"Really, I'm fine. I don't think the angels expected me to succeed - they didn't even put me in a magic proofed room."

"Well of course not you silly human mage." Furcifer teased her. "But why didn't you contact me? I mean an orgy cannot have taken preference over letting your faction know you're safe!"

"It was a threesome, and I don't know about that." She stretched out.

"You have a girlfriend, Manon!" Furcifer groaned.

"I asked for permission." She protested.

"So... You've been back long enough to ask your girlfriend for permission for a threesome, have said threesome, but not to let us know you were ok?" Furcifer said.

"Look. I found out about the time thing, Kaoru told me. I wanted to adjust and make sure I was ok before I was called in to answer a lot of questions. Don't tell me you wouldn't have had me questioned as soon as I walked in. Don't pretend you would have stood ready with a blanket and hot cocoa."

"Stop mentioning hot cocoa." Lydia groaned. "Been a long time, Manon." She smiled, happy to change the subject.

"Yeah! I had no idea you were helping out! I would have just texted you where I was!" She smiled.

"Oh I thought I was just tracking the angel. But we should go see that new rom com together, I really can't convince Twitch."

"Yeah of course!" Smiled Manon.

Furcifer sighed. "Focus, please!" Manon's comment had stung, but she was right. He was deadly curious. "When you're ready, maybe we can go home."

Kaoru sat up. "Let the girl recover a bit." He said simply. "She did travel dimensions less than an hour ago."

"So that's why you touched her with your dickwand, to make her all better?" Furcifer bit. "I thought -"

"What, you thought angels were all chaste and good? I have just as much of an agenda as you do." Kaoru glared over, letting the ladies have the blanket so they could scoot to the bathroom.

"What is that agenda, then?" Furcifer asked, crouching down.

"To be happy, simply put. The ladies wanted to spend time, I spent time with them. Manon didn't want me to call you, so I let her decide to do so on her own time. Maybe you should learn from that." The angel sat there, completely naked, almost half of Furcifer's height, and he still scared him. It was his composure, his cool that made Furcifer break out in goosebumps.

Furcifer sighed. He needed to calm down. Yes, it hurt that Manon had not come straight to him, but she had explained why. Any more fighting would only make things worse. As the bathroom door closed, Furcifer sat down.

"How did you know to try and make a portal to get Manon home?"

"I didn't. I was just trying to make a portal to gauge my power when it suddenly connected. It exhausted me to no end to keep it open – and even so she did lose an inch of hair because I couldn't keep the portal open as long as I should." He took a deep breath.

Furcifer nodded. That was to be expected.

"How are your energy levels?" He wondered.

"Low. I had to push myself. It'll be a few more days before I can help you open the portal to the other world. I doubt the council will make a move before then."

"They already have." Furcifer said, before bringing him up to date with all that had happened – the theft of his notes, the attack in the hallway.

"Oh wow." Kaoru said, impressed. "I'm sorry that happened to you." He shook his head. "There must be something here they want. Did they steal any books about your world?"

"Now that you mention it... I did lose a few history books. I just assumed they had been destroyed or taken by accident." Furcifer said. "You think they mean to learn about our world?"

"The council is comprised of mostly merchants." Kaoru

sighed. "They would want to know what kind of trade they could do with this world."

"I hope that's it." He blinked when Kaoru gave him a confused look. "Oh you know, in all the alien movies when the alien invaders gather info about the planet they're invading, it's to find out how they can destroy it."

"But we're not invading...?" Kaoru looked confused.

"Yeah, never mind." Furcifer laughed, looking up when the ladies came back, dressed.

"Manon? Do you want to go home?" Furcifer asked her.

Manon considered it a moment, then nodded. "Yeah. Yeah, I'd like that." She pushed some of her hair behind her ears. "Just... Please don't interrogate me until tomorrow? I'm still trying to figure out how I'm going to explain away just vanishing for days."

"Write it down if you need to. Then you can just send me through what you want." Said Furcifer. "Kaoru, is there any chance they are coming back for her?"

"Maybe. She was probably interrogated about this world. But they would find other ways to find out." He shrugged. "The council is not a bunch of kidnappers and thugs, they're ..."

"Believing they're doing right for their own world." Furcifer nodded. It was nice to be reminded. For all that had happened, he worried that he was seeing the other side as bad guys automatically. Something that would not work in his favour if he had to negotiate treaties with them in the near future. Perhaps he would have to abstain – it was very likely they would still be discussing laws at this point. To Furcifer, it was only a matter of days before both sides acknowledged one another and a reliable portalway was established, so that they could communicated and hopefully solve all differences between them. This backwards way of dealing with one another had to stop soon before they ended up in trouble.

Manon took a deep breath. "Let's go then." She smiled a little and looked over. "I can't wait to sleep in my own room." She winced a bit as she walked forward.

Furcifer just shook his head. "Oh! Kaoru, meet my friend Lydia, she's Twitch's... girl... friend?"

"Yes." Lydia smiled and held a hand out.

Kaoru stood up and shook her hand, before pressing a soft kiss to it.

"It's an honour to meet you." He replied. "I'm guessing your power is the reason they found me?"

"I just scryed." She blushed.

"It's a great talent, miss Lydia, treasure it." He said and let go of her hand.

"I do." She replied, pulling her hand back and putting an arm around Twitch's waist. "We should get going."

Twitch nodded. "Yeah. You need a rest and that hot

cocoa."

Furcifer nodded. "Let me give you a ride back." He said. "It's the least I can do." He pulled his phone out and called headquarters to send out a car. He'd not owned a car ever since returning, so he mostly depended on the transportation provided by the faction and general public transport. His license had long expired and he wasn't even sure he would renew it. It had become so useless recently so he didn't mind either way.

Twitch looked over. "Thanks. I completely lost track of where we are."

"We're near the outskirts of town. It's about a thirty minute ride to get back to the centre of town - twenty five if you want to go to the Elite headquarters."

"No thanks." Twitch said coolly. "City centre is fine."

Lydia nodded. "Yeah, I agree. There's a chocolate bar in the centre that does amazing white hot chocolate... And caramel hot chocolate. And creamy baileys hot chocolate."

"Aaand now I want hot chocolate." Furcifer shook his head. "Come on." He walked outside to wait for the car. He'd seen enough for today. He doubted that Kaoru wanted to come home with him.

Kaoru joined him outside, wrapped in a blanket and in fuzzy slippers. "Thank you." He said.

"For what?" Furcifer asked.

Kaoru shrugged. "You did come to find me, with limited

company. You didn't come here with your whole faction or anything, and I appreciate it. Just... Oh well. Take care of Manon." He nodded.

Furcifer nodded. "Of course." He peeked over to the woman, who was climbing into the car.

"And put some clothes on, Kaoru. Just so you know. Your son was at Aiden's." He shook his head. That boy needed to figure out how to live in the human world properly. He could already see some of the neighbours peek out of their windows to see what was going on. It seemed a quiet neighbourhood – not the kind where a bunch of strangers suddenly showed up. One of them being an angel was definitely a rare occurrence.

Furcifer sighed and got into the car with Manon, Twitch and Lydia. The driver looked around. "Furcifer, right? City centre. I'll drop you off by the mall." He said with a little nod, making sure everyone was buckled up before taking off.

Manon seemed absent, quiet, staring out the window. Furcifer shook his head. Perhaps she just needed some time, a bit of peace and quiet to find herself again and to organise her thoughts. She had just been somewhere where no human had gone before.

The car ride was awkward at best. The first few blocks, it was silent – Manon had not said a word since leaving the angel's residence. She did not seem upset either, but her mood worried Furcifer, who was used to her energetic personality bubbling, begging to be heard.

Twitch and Lydia were happy to fill the silence in the car. Lydia especially was happy to have found that her spell was working and was talking about all the little aspects and features she had added to make it work properly. She got a little smile and a nod from Manon. It seemed, without the distraction the angel had happily provided, she was lost in thoughts and worries.

Furcifer was happy Twitch and Lydia were trying to quell the awkwardness, but they once they had been dropped off where their wild hunt had started, it was quiet again. At this point Furcifer knew better than to try and start a conversation.

It didn't get much better after arriving at the building. She trekked almost straight to her room, after briefly hugging Gabrielle and exchanging a few whispered words.

Gabrielle walked over, arms crossed. Not a good sign.

"What's up?" He asked, looking over Gabrielle, trying to read her.

"She's somewhat upset with you." Gabrielle said. "Let me guess, she didn't call you right away and you got all uppity about it?"

"Yeah. But I feel that's my right. She can't just – vanish and reappear and not let me know!" He shook his head. "That's just rude."

"It's not rude when she's trying to preserve her own sanity. She's got non magical friends and family who she'll have to explain to why she vanished, who will get all over her. You never even considered that, did you?" She shook her head.

"No... I was thinking about myself. But when do I ever think about anyone else, Gabrielle?" He asked with a sigh. "I just wanted to talk to her about how it was over there."

"You'll have to wait." She shook her head. "She's asked me to contact her family and to let her know she's safe and will contact her soon. And until she gets back to her feet, you don't even think about talking to her."

"Can I at least ask her to note everything down?"

"No!" Gabrielle threw her hands up. "I get that you're excited. But you don't get an automatic pass to her and her time. She will not have forgotten any of this in a few days."

"Fine." He sighed and held his hands up in a gesture of agreement. "I'll wait for her to come to me. How's that?"

"That's all I'm asking you." Said Gabrielle. "Thanks. Now go get some rest."

Furcifer nodded, patting her shoulder before taking the elevator up to his temporary quarters. He could do with some downtime, a bit of a rest. A moment to gather his thoughts.

Chapter 30

It was the middle of the night when Furcifer startled awake. He sat up straight, taking a deep breath. In his dream, the attack had featured - but this time, there had been no handy stairwell, and he had been running, running, without finding a way to escape the assailants heading his way. There were seven of them, carrying heavy clubs and weapons, and no matter how fast he ran, they steadily caught up with him. There was no getting away from them. As he ran, the world was being torn apart.

Furcifer stared at his hands and took deep breaths to calm himself down. A lot had gone on since Manon had come back from the angel world. In the few days since the portal incident, residents had reported strange distortions - as if the portal was sapping reality still. Items vanished in small, spontaneous portals, only to reappear in a neighbour's home. Cats who found themselves in other people's attics and children who dared their friends to stick a head through one of those spontaneous portals to see where they lead. While it seemed the outcomes of the portals had been confined to the block where Kaoru's wife lived, they were still extremely disruptive. Immediately, the authorities had forbid any more portaling in the city, much to the dislike of many of the mages there. Not to mention the measure would not help much – it didn't stop the angels from creating portals to get here. Hell, for all they knew these spontaneous portals were not so much a rip in reality as clumsy attempts from the angelic side to try and contact them. Furcifer finally got up, shakily, and moved to the bathroom to pee. Perhaps that would help him regain his wits.

The portal ban had caused more inconvenience than just mages having to take the bus to work. It meant Gareth had to stop all experiments, even his regular portal studies, and had had to hand over everything to the authorities to be studied by a "selected committee of mages". This worried Furcifer, not in the least because neither he nor Gareth had been selected for this fancy committee. It was shrouded in mystery, which lead Furcifer to believe one faction had wormed their way into a good position in the government, possibly through the MLAE. That explanation would make the most sense – the selected mages would not be able to disclose they were on the committee. The government would not want the mage community to know they were preferring one faction over the others, of course. Best case, the committee had been set up to contain mages from all factions, but he had not been selected because of his bias in the matter. There would be indeed no way he would not fight for the use of portals – how else was he going to get anywhere?

Furcifer flushed and ambled back to the bed. There was no way he was going to let this happen without a fight. The more time passed in this insecurity, the more time the angels had to interpret it as a hostile action. This could not end well for either side. They either started a war or Kaoru never got home.

The Summerfest celebration to the goddess Alorna would have been the day before and his absence there would have been noticed, Kaoru had told him. He'd thought he would have been back by then. But without him there it would give the council the ability to replace him. Even if it was temporary, they would be able to reverse a lot of the laws he had installed to make his kingdom more progressive. To reinstate them again would be a battle. It was easy for a government to pretend it was acting on the behalf of the people when the people were distracted by their lost, popular king.

It was not a good situation. Furcifer crawled back into bed and closed his eyes. Though he tried to think about everything but the angels, they wormed his way back into his head. He had a meeting with Gabrielle and Manon about her experiences in the other world, so he really wanted to get enough sleep so he could do the interview properly. He took a deep breath and turned around, closing his eyes as he tried to get some sleep. It didn't come – he just found his thoughts drifting back and forth again, never being able to let go and clear his mind. Finally he gave up. A glance at the clock told him it was five am, so he got up. It was no use agonising in bed if he couldn't get any sleep after all. He started on some tea and turned on the lights in his room. To retrieve his notes he would have to walk into the hallway, so he preferred waiting until he was awake enough to remember to bring keys. Last thing he wanted was to wake up the janitor because he had forgotten his keys – she would never let him live that one down. He picked up his notes with the questions he had wanted to ask Kaoru while he was in the hospital and struck through every question he now had an answer to. It only took about half of the questions off of the list, and even with that selection he doubted she would have an answer to all of them. He sighed and went to pour himself a cup of tea. Now what was he going to do?

He shook his head and sat down with the cup, looking over the mess of notes gathered on his desk. There were just the items he considered the minimum for his work – his own notes, not the processed results. Still, lately he had been careful to keep a copy of everything in the central hub, just so nothing could be stolen easily. Sure, stuff could happen. The cleaners could try and organise his room and accidentally throw out everything. The central hub could get stuck and become inaccessible. But nobody was stealing his work again. He took a deep breath and started on a new list of questions to ask. That way he could let Gabrielle look over it, and see if she was okay with the questions.

It would show her he wasn't just shooting from the hip here – he had an actual plan for this. He really wanted to make sure this went well. His relationship with Manon could suffer if he did not do this right.

No pressure. No pressure at all. He sighed to himself and threw away the page he had been writing on, staring at a white page. This was hard. For a change he had to think about how he posed these questions. Manon was not just anyone – she had possibly been traumatised by all of this. There was no saying what she had seen on the other side. The angels seemed peaceful, but their definition of peaceful could be different. There had to be a reason she was so upset to be coming back. Perhaps... No, she would have told them if it was something serious. Gabrielle had been sticking close to her, and had kept her up to date about the developments. If there was something that was urgent, or time sensitive, she would have told them. Maybe it had really just been the time away that had made her so morose. He sighed and stared at the blank page in front of him. It just would not come. He realised that there weren't any exact questions he wanted to ask her – he wanted to make sure she was ok and let her tell her story.

"What happened..." He mouthed as he wrote down. That was a good start. He looked proudly at that question and sipped some more tea.

Chapter 31

It was ten am when he suddenly woke up, ink on his face and his pages of notes scattered.

"Not today..." He muttered, sitting up and pulling his hair out of his face. "Fuck." He checked the clock. This waking up on top of books was becoming a habit.

His meeting with Gabrielle and Manon was in an hour. Immediately energised, he rushed to the shower to get ready. His list of questions had not come about in the end, but he could live with that. He would just let her take the lead and let her tell him what she wanted to say. That would probably be the best approach. He took a deep breath as he turned on the water and let it run over him. He had to be more like that - let go of control a little, flow with what was happening. Otherwise he risked being left behind. With a sigh he ran a hand through his wet hair and started washing up.

In a way it was a blessing he had fallen asleep on his notes. Getting some sleep was better than agonising over the questions for hours then going to the meeting half asleep with overly complex questions. At least, that was what he was trying to tell himself. He felt somewhat stupid that despite the ages he had taken to prepare, he would go in half cocked. There was nothing he could do about that now, except make sure he was there on time. He checked the clock and cursed- he was wasting way too much time on this shower. He turned off the tap and got out.

It wasn't any kind of special occasion, but he decided to dress up a bit. He donned a nice button up shirt, a v-neck sweater and some dress pants. At the very least he would look the part.

He made his way down to the lobby. Because of the recent security issues they had decided to hold the meeting within the building, with security nearby. Joe, not used to just standing still, stood by the entrance to the meeting room nervously, weight shifting from foot to foot.

"You alright there?" Furcifer asked. He had to admit he was considering the man a friend after all that had happened.

Joe nodded his head. "Gareth helped me out. I'm still writing the report, but I'm sure Gareth will brief you if you ask him."

Furcifer shrugged. "Just finish the report."

He said, patting the man on the shoulder before entering. Gareth had been a nervous ball of energy after having been told he could not continue his study of the portals. Assigning him to help out Joe had been good, the mage had time to spare and energy enough to get to the bottom of what had happened.

Furcifer took a deep breath before walking into the room.

"Hi." He nodded to Gabrielle and Manon. They were sitting around a small round table, both clutching a mug of coffee.

Gabrielle looked up first. From here he could see it wasn't actually coffee in Manon's mug, but hot chocolate. The smell made him very aware of his growling stomach. When had he eaten last?

"Furcifer. Hi." She smiled a little. Manon looked up as well.

"Hey." Manon looked up. He only realised it now, but she looked again like her old self. When he had picked her up she was pale and tired looking – she had gotten some colour back in her face.

"How've you been?" Furcifer asked.

Manon nodded. "Good. I saw my family yesterday." She said. "I told them I had gone on an unplanned study trip about magic and that I had forgotten my phone charger. They believed it."

"Well, you're a model daughter. I bet this is only the first time or so you've ever gone missing unexpectedly."

She laughed. "That's not a credit to most people!" She shook her head. "Thanks though. I know you would have backed up my story had they called."

"Of course." He shook his head. "It was kind of my fault you ended up there."

"No it wasn't." She raised an eyebrow. "It was... Look, it wasn't as if I was kidnapped. What happened is that..." She cleared her throat. "I saw them come through the portal and hid. It wasn't hard, I don't think they were looking for me so I just jumped onto a bed and closed the curtain around it when I heard the portal open. They.... Looked around for a bit and just talked to one another before vanishing back into the portal. It was still open so I... I went after them." She smiled a little. "I mean can you blame me? You always told me to take the opportunity when it presents itself."

Furcifer sighed and looked over. She was right – and he would probably have done the same thing if he had been there. But this was a dangerous thing to do! He was about to reprimand her when he realised that wasn't the point of the meeting.

"Go on." He encouraged.

Manon cleared her throat and sipped some more hot chocolate.

"I didn't believe it at first. I was so sure they had just portalled from outside or something, not directly from the angel kingdom. It was... weird." She laughed a little. "The grass - it was purple. That's the first thing I saw. There was a castle, huge and white, and I could still see the angels walk to it. I panicked and tried to go back, but the portal had closed. And at that point I realised how stupid I had been to just - dive through a portal into fuck knows where." She shook her head and stared down into her mug.

"You did alright." He reached out and touched her hand. "Now don't dwell, you were getting to the good part." He said, only half joking. Gabrielle's annoyed face shut him up. Manon cleared her throat.

"Right, right... So I was out there, like half a mile away from the castle. I was not sure where to go - there was a hill and when I climbed it I saw a village, just a few miles away. Oh, there was also a village right outside of the castle." She bit her lip as she focussed on describing it. "It was... strange. It wasn't like - you'd think medieval times or something. But no. The buildings were modern and there were proper roads and everyone looked well dressed and healthy and there were stands with fruits and vegetables but nobody seemed to pay, they just... took." She sighed. "At that point I was getting hungry and tired, so I thought I'd sneak to the village, but..." She pointed at her back.

"It was pretty obvious I'm not an angel, you know? But there were others without wings so I thought if I could just... look confident enough I would just waltz in, take some fruit and then try and hide in the forest until someone portaled away. I mean, considering they portaled so far away from the castle there could have been some wards." She shrugged.

"I was just about to enter the village when I was stopped by Mammon. Uh, he's uh, head of Kaoru's halfling army. Tower of a man. Beautiful wings, like feathery wings covered in a thin layer of leather. He told me he was the head of the guards and asked me who I was, and I tried lying, but he saw through it, so he just... took me into the castle. I wasn't a prisoner or anything. They just... gave me shelter and food and fresh clothes so I would fit in a bit more. They said that if anyone asked, to tell them I was under the arrest of the royal guard. That freaked me out a little, until I learned that the council was just salivating to get their hands on me. Mammon protected me and to keep them quiet, he asked me for bits of information to pass on to them. That way it seemed like I was cooperating." She looked into the mug.

Furcifer shivered at that. That almost mirrored what they were doing with Kaoru here, not keeping him prisoner, but demanding information regardless.

"The first few days it was fine. Nobody even looked at me without Mammon warning them. He did not let me out of his sight when I was outside." She licked her lips. "But that only counts for so much, you know? Ah, I'm – I'm going to get some coffee, want any?"

Furcifer groaned. "It just got good..."

"Furcifer." Gabrielle said softly.

Furcifer swallowed. "Yes. I'd love some tea." He nodded and got up to prepare some. The meeting room had an electric kettle and some instant coffee, tea bags, sugar and cups of milk to make their hot drinks. Furcifer turned his nose up at the instant coffee and picked out a teabag.

"Gabrielle?" He peeked back at her.

Gabrielle raised her mug. "I'm good."

"Thanks for being so patient." Whispered Manon. "I mean... This has been crazy."

Furcifer could see her hands trembling a bit as she poured some instant coffee into her mug.

"Yeah." Furcifer agreed. "I mean... Kaoru told me a lot about his world and the trade system, but he obviously does not know much about the life outside of the court. I would give an arm and a leg to see that village." He took a deep breath and shook his head as the kettle turned off. "Okay, maybe not an arm and a leg. A few toes." The rolling boil of the kettle made him look up again.

"You first, ma'am." He poured some water on top of the instant coffee she had heaped into the mug and smiled.

"Thanks. They didn't have black tea, by the way. Just green and jasmine and all of that."

"I take back what I said, this is the best of all possible worlds."

Manon laughed at that, covering her mouth. "You would still totally go."

"Only if I could take a stash of English Breakfast."

"Sure." She looked over, a twinkle in her eyes, and Furcifer was glad to see the old Manon was returning to her own self.

"So what happened that you tried to escape?" He asked. "I thought Mammon was protecting you."

"Yeah. But to the council he's just a half blood. Kaoru gave a lot of the half bloods status by deeming them worthy of being his personal guards, but that doesn't mean the rest of society agrees with that decision." She looked over. "He's a good man, Kaoru."

"So people keep telling me." Shrugged Furcifer. "But I don't trust him. Not yet." He moved the electric kettle to pour some onto his tea bag before replacing the kettle.

"You have issues." Manon walked back to the table.

Furcifer shrugged, walking back as well. "Do you feel like continuing?"

"Yeah." She sat down with the coffee and looked over to Gabrielle. "So uh... What happened was that the council was trying to overrule Mammon. They kept trying to claim that because I had come through the portal with them I was in their custody, and the court seemed to be on their side. Without Kaoru there, the court basically rules." She explained, looking from Furcifer to Gabrielle.

"So it's important he gets back soon." Nodded Furcifer. "How about your return, how did you manage that?" He had heard Kaoru's side, but not hers.
"Well... I – I know how it started. Mammon had told me a few hours prior he would not be able to protect me much longer. The council would want me delivered to them the next morning. I was so scared! There were no real wards on my room, so... I tried. I just tried making a portal and suddenly, it shifted. You know when you start a portal and it seems to dig through reality, to form a straight tunnel to where you want to go? It felt like that at first but then it jerked to the right, and suddenly, it... It connected. I could see Kaoru, but I could also see a normal human house, so I just bolted. The rest you know." She smiled a little, sadly. "Now I wish I'd spent more time on that side, had done some more exploring... But it is what it is."

Furcifer shook his head. "You were smart not to go too far. But I'm happy you told me everything." He sipped his tea and looked over. "How do you feel?"

"Still tired. Gareth told me it could be because the angel world has another kind of magic stream, like... It takes a lot out of you to be there." She put her hand up a little, finding it hard to describe. "Also. It was like... three days on that end."

"That would make sense. If their magic developed differently from ours it would only make sense." He admitted. "I can imagine someone from our world not lasting very long there." He sighed and shook his head.

"Nope. And that's where we have a problem." Said Gabrielle. "We have some info. It looks like the magic drought may be over. This year's magic wave is set to hit somewhere this week. If Kaoru is still here, it might affect the magic of everyone who is born into new powers."

"What do you mean?" Furcifer asked, not sure where she was going with this.

"A whole generation of mages may be unable to survive earth." She looked up.

Furcifer had had to let that all sink in as he made his way to Aiden's. He'd learned a lot from both Manon's story and what little Kaoru had told him. If he was going to do this, break the law again, he was going to figure out all there was to know.

For a weekday, the mall was crowded. People doing their usual shopping, mostly, but to his horror Furcifer saw the crowds extended to Aiden's store.

He pushed his way in and to the counter, where Russell and Aiden were running back and forth.

"What's going on? Flash sale?"

"Funny." Aiden made a face and turned away to fill an order. "People are worried this ban means there won't be any magic allowed and are stocking up on protection spells and charms. There's... been many people unhappy about magic users."

That was an understatement. Pretty much every news report had some magic experts talking about the portal ban or any occurrences around the city they thought had to so with magic. Crime up? Magic.

"Can I talk to..." He made a hand gesture.

"Yeah, sure." Scoffed Aiden, not too happy the other didn't even seem to care about his issues. Furcifer did, but he also had the knowledge that the sooner he solved this, the better it would be for everyone. He slinked behind the counter and walked into the back, looking around for the angel.

"We need to talk."

Kaoru sat up and yawned. "Shoot. I'm guessing it has to do with why the front is so busy." He said.

"Indeed." Furcifer walked to the kitchen to help himself to some tea."Tea?"

Chapter 32

Furcifer sat back, trying to wrap his head around what had just been said.

"That's bad." He said, looking over. "How sure is this wave?"

"Pretty sure." Gabrielle fished out her own notebook. "The Scribe's pattern finders predicted it for this month. We're in the last week of that time span." She looked up. "We've been keeping an eye out to make sure we didn't miss it, and it hasn't happened." She looked up.

Furcifer sighed and rubbed his chin. "This is only the first the Scribes have been able to predict a wave, right?"

"Yeah. We don't even quite know how it works yet but it does." She looked up to him. "It involves more math than a liberal arts professor like you would know what to do with, but we know it's coming."

Furcifer stalled for time by sipping his tea. He knew about the prediction department - they had been working on predicting and seeing patterns in the waves of magic that happened. First they had established they were often only every two years by interviewing mages to establish when they had gained their powers. That had given them a good indication of the regularity of the phenomenon. To predict it from that was complex but possible – there were certain energy signatures that preceded these waves. More precisely, there would be storms where magical things would happen like new trees appearing and thunderbolts changing colour. About a month after such a storm, a wave of magic would hit. Predicting those storms had been the hard part.

It was theorised the storm consumed magic as much as it expelled it, and that the absorbed energy was released again in the magic wave. If so, Kaoru's large magical power would definitely be absorbed, leaving the angel weaker and their next generation of mages affected.

He thought about Oni. She had already some power, but the wave would definitely affect her. She was still early in her magical development.

"We can't postpone it." He shook his head. "Then we best get the angel out of here."
"How? We can't even portal in the city." Manon shook her head. "And we can't take him out of the city – he would be noticed."
She was right. Every other form of transport would risk

the angel being spotted and found. Even if they stuffed him into a van, it would be risky.

"It's our best shot. We can't risk an entire generation of mages for the sake of obeying the law." He looked over. "We need to plan it, yes, but I believe we can get away with it." There had been so many times they had done something that they should not have. He found it hard to see the danger in it now.

Gabrielle sighed. "That's what you said last time."

"You don't get to comment on that, miss Let-me-hide-some-bangles-to-find-Furcifer-the-greatest-mage-of-all."

"Yeah, nobody would call you the greatest mage of all." Gabrielle raised an eyebrow. "But alright. I'll work with you on this. It's all we can do. If being in the angel world has an effect on humans, the reverse might be true as well. Even if he himself does not notice it Kaoru might be weakening."

Furcifer nodded. "Very likely. Because he is injured he might not even have noticed himself." He sighed and looked down at the empty cup of tea.

"Alright. See if Gareth is up for some mischief - he will have the best chance of creating a portal." He got up to make more tea.

"They took his notes, Furcifer." Gabrielle looked over. "And we're done here."

"He's got a super advanced tablet that looks like he could fire rockets from it. I'm sure he has backups.

Besides, what do I keep telling people?" He waved his hand.

"Write it down then digitise it." Manon chuckled. She had heard that line so often.

"He does photograph every page he writes." She looked to Gabrielle, who looked impressed.

"No wonder you take so long for everything." Gabrielle glanced over to Furcifer. "So let's see what he's got left then." She got up and walked to the exit of the meeting room.

Furcifer chuckled. "I impressed you." He teased, abandoning his tea making plans to open the door for her.

"Did not." She looked over. "I'm not impressed you tell people to make backups."

"You aa-aaare." he chanted, holding the door for her.

"Fine, if it'll shut you up, I'm impressed. It's quite a sensible idea I had not expected from you."

"Thank you. That's all I wanted to hear." He bowed.

Gabrielle shook her head. "I cannot believe I almost married you."

"I cannot believe you let a catch like me go." He winked. His mood had definitely improved from that conversation. One thing he hated was the routine of complacency he had settled in, where taking time to study his own things had become a rebellious act.

Manon shook her head. "Hey, did anyone even bother

to check whether I want to be involved in something criminal?"

Furcifer looked over. "Because I didn't assume you would be involved." He said honestly. "I think you've been through enough."

"Thank you." She smiled, happy to be excluded. "Word of warning though. It seems going through a portal erases any magic cast on yourself in this world."

"So wards don't work." Furcifer looked over.

"And would possibly backfire." Gabrielle looked over. "So best to go in as clear minded as possible."

Furcifer sighed. "Ugh. I don't trust that." He shook his head. "Alright then. Let's go formulate a plan." He said, looking over to Manon.

"You, you relax out here. Go to your family or whatever." He sighed and took Manon's hand briefly. It was still warm from the cup of coffee.

"Who are you taking?" She asked. Clearly, she was not going to fight his decision, but he could understand she was interested.

"Gabrielle. Gareth. Twitch and or Aiden. And Kaoru, obviously." He licked his lips. "The gang, basically."

"I refuse to be in any gang with you." Sighed Gabrielle. "But yeah. I'll go with. Someone needs to keep you in check." She shrugged and looked over.

"Good." Furcifer nodded. "Greatly appreciated. "I'll feel a lot better to have you there." He had to admit. It wasn't so much a matter of having another mage, but to have one he could trust there. Especially if they would be unable to ward off any attacks, having someone to watch his back would be very handy. She was a gifted mage and a good fighter – she would come in more than useful. Gareth would be there to do the portalling and advanced portalling magic. Aiden or Twitch would prove to be great back up with their generalised magic. And they knew how to handle themselves.

Furcifer walked out and towards the elevator. At least Gareth would be happy to be able to work on portals again. Of course it would not be legal, but the faction had a legal team just for these kinds of things. Nothing too much to worry about there. And by the time anyone found out, Kaoru would at least be safe and home. And the latest generation of mages would have nothing to fear except for their own angst.

"Alright then. Let's go see Gareth." Gabrielle shrugged. "He'll be doubly happy to have some work again. We've been keeping him busy with some studies and reports, but he'll be delighted to do portal magic again."

"I just hope he kept the backups." Furcifer sighed. Sure, he'd been full of bravado about the backups thing, but he had no idea if the young mage had actually kept the backups or handed them over when the authorities asked for them.

Gabrielle groaned. "For once I hope you're right." She walked to the elevator and jabbed the button. Furcifer took her in. Her silver hair made it hard to guess her age, and her body was well trained with visible muscles. She usually wore some kind of chainmail, and today was no exception – her sleeves had a line of the metal rings, extending into her cuffs. It was not just a stylistic choice – metal was a conductor and it helped her direct magic, the line of metal acting like a wand. It saved her a lot of time and effort in spells.

He shuffled into the elevator after her, catching a whiff of her perfume. An old fashioned scent, so contrasting her modern style.

As the doors of the elevator opened on Gareth's floor, they were greeted with a wave of sound – some kind of loud techno music which assaulted their ears.

"I think he's in." Gabrielle said with a little smirk.

"What?" Furcifer wasn't sure he'd heard her. They walked to the door and knocked loudly.

Instantly, the music was turned off and the door was opened.

"Too loud?"

"I'll let you know when my hearing returns." Furcifer grumped, looking over to the boy. He looked even more unkempt as usual, confirming his suspicion that the boy mainly showered and dressed in clean clothes to go out and present his ideas to others. When his research had been paused, it seemed his routine had as well.

"When's the last time you had a shower? Loud techno raves don't substitute for hygiene." Furcifer waved a hand.

Gareth grinned. "Star Trek has sonic showers, but fine, I'll shower tonight. So uh, any news?" He asked, letting them walk into the little flat.

Furcifer looked around. It was a little neater than usual, but not by much.

Gabrielle turned to face the boy mage. "We need a portal to the other world." She simply said, never one to stretch the fun out. Sad, Furcifer thought.

"Yes!" Gareth wooped as he dropped onto his office chair and spun around. "I mean, oh sure. But what about the ban?"

"The ban is still in place." Gabrielle conceded. "But we have a bigger problem. Kaoru's presence here may influence the magic of all new mages on earth if he remains. That's why we need to bring him back, as soon as we can."

"Of course." Gareth seemed to have only half listened to her explanation as he was already busy gathering his materials from various hiding spots. Furcifer proudly saw that he had kept backups – several tablets came out of hiding and were turned on.

"So what do you need?" Furcifer asked, craning his neck to peek at the tablet computers. The writing was incomprehensible. Long strings of words and phrases he was unfamiliar with.

"Well..." He thought and took a deep breath. "It's easiest to do it in a location where it has been done before."

Furcifer nodded. "Agnes' house."

"Negative." Gabrielle said. "It wasn't a portal - that was a convergence of two separate portal spells creating a portal. And even if we did it we will end up where Manon was, which seemed to have been some sort of well-guarded room. I don't want to end up in a room next to general Mammon."

"He might be on our side... or he was just on Manon's." Furcifer begrudgingly admitted. "But Kaoru will know a spot. He's done the crossing multiple times. So consider that sorted. What else?"

"Pheeeww... I would need to test it once or twice before we do it." Gareth looked up.

"No." Furcifer shook his head. "If Kaoru's spot is in public, people will be itchy to report any kind of strange goings-on off the portal variety. Best to just do it in one fast go if possible."

Gareth sighed. "You're not making this easy." His enthusiasm seemed to make way for reality, which Furcifer appreciated.

"It's not meant to be easy."

"True!" Gareth regained his wide grin and looked over. "True. Oh gosh this is exciting!"

"It's not a disaster if it doesn't work the first time, but try and make sure we can try again quickly. How much time would you need to get this show on the road?"

"Give me a day to dust off the magic knowledge." He smiled and looked over the tablet computers, scrolling through documents. "But I can have it ready for you... tomorrow night."

Furcifer looked over to Gabrielle. "That sound alright to you? I think middle of the night might be our best option."

Gabrielle tutted her lips but then nodded. "Alright." She said. "Cover of night will be safest. Just remember books are hard to read in the dark."

"Torches are cheap." Furcifer looked over with a shrug. "And this is quite exciting."

"I have to admit there's a certain thrill to it." Gabrielle crossed her arms. "Is this how you feel all the time?"

"Of course not. That would make it boring." Furcifer chuckled and blinked as he was handed a little piece of paper.

"What's this?" He asked.

"Stuff I'll need. Aiden might have it, but some things will need to be ordered so call ahead." He looked up.

"Sure..." Frowned Furcifer. "This stuff is expensive."

"Take it out of my allowance, and get double of everything!" The boy said excitedly.

Furcifer looked over to Gabrielle. "I've created a monster."

"Don't be silly." She chuckled. "You merely gave the monster a safer place to haunt."

Chapter 33

Furcifer was already exhausted physically. They had left Gareth's an hour or so later to go buy the items from Aiden, but they had been advised not to use any magic. They would need to conserve as much of their energy as needed. Not to mention not all ingredients were stable.

Furcifer shifted the shopping bags in his hands. "You're walking too fast! Slow down!"
Gabrielle reluctantly slowed down. "Well. I've told you before to exercise more." Despite the fact she was carrying even more bags than him, she hadn't even broken a sweat.
"Yeah right, can you see me in bicycle shorts?" Furcifer made a face.
"I try not to." She had to admit, turning back to start walking again. "I try not to think about you too much if possible."
"Harsh." He shook his head. "But probably for the best."
Gabrielle sighed. "Yeah. Probably." Still, she slowed down.

He didn't really want to talk about this yet – they could never go back to what they once were. Their needs were too different.

"Have you considered..." She glanced over. "A relationship?"

"With...?" He gave her a confused look.

"Things have been over between us for a while. You never went on another date. Are you over me?" She glanced over. Perhaps this was something he shouldn't have put off for so long.

"I am." He glanced over. "I just don't think I'll have what we had with anyone else."

"Oh no don't-"

"That's not meant to guilt you in any way." He made a face. "I've not had sex since we broke up. I've not felt the need. I realised early on you were the one to always start so I made a move a few times. But I just don't feel that need." He glanced over. "I could do with a relationship. I would. I miss what we had. What I don't miss is the sex." He took a deep breath. This was a lot of his own feelings, laid bare. But if he couldn't tell her... Despite all of this she was still his best friend.

If she didn't understand, she was making a good effort to hide it. He could see her look, perhaps a bit puzzled, but understanding.

"Well. Maybe if your ego was a little smaller." She deviated from the depth of their conversation. It made him chuckle.

"So where's the car?" He peered around.

"Other side of the parking lot." Gabrielle flexed her arms and smiled. "It's not far, come on. You need to do some cardio."

"I hate that word."

"Alright." She cast a spell to lighten the load he carried a bit and walked towards the car. All of the unstable ingredients were in her bag, but it was still a bit risky.

"I think we got everything he asked for..." She popped the trunk with a button on her key and peeked at the list in her hand. "Yup!"

"Thanks." He grudgingly said, feeling the load being much more manageable all of a sudden.

"No worries." She popped the items into her boot and sighed. "So. do you think this is it? These are all the ingredients someone needs to go into a whole different world?" She asked, looking over to the items in her boot.

"Well I'm not so sure about the hot pockets. But the rest seems about right." He nodded, looking over to it. It was quite the mixture of herbs and potions, even some which Aiden had had to look up and then prepare in a hurry. They didn't have much time, after all. Nevertheless he trusted Aiden. His working ethic was impeccable when it came to the store.

"We still need to let Kaoru in on the plan." Gabrielle looked over.

"Not yet. He's got his own agenda and I don't want to alert him until the moment where we have the plan ready to go. He might just decide he doesn't want to inconvenience us and scram, which would be utterly useless to us." He shook his head. "We cannot trust him."

Gabrielle walked to the driver's seat. "You need to trust someone."

"I trust you. Somewhat." He was only half joking, knowing that in the end his agenda was his own. Gabrielle was determined to keep the factions alive – he just wanted to gain knowledge and survive. Anything else was superfluous. If it came to having to destroy the faction system to get more knowledge, he would do it in a heartbeat. For now, it worked out for his personal agenda - an agenda which had changed over time, he had to admit. He could live with being a faction leader now. It was a necessary evil.

"Let's get home." Gabrielle slipped into the car and looked over. "Thanks for your help on this."

"My help on this? I thought of the whole thing." He scoffed and got into the passenger side seat. Her car was roomy and clean, not often used.

Gabrielle rolled her eyes. "You know what I mean. For once you didn't completely start this mess but you're willing to help out. That's big." She said, looking over.

He sighed and slipped into the car. "Whatever, cupcake. Let's go." He said, looking forward to getting back to the tower. It was a kind of safety blanket now that portals had been outlawed in the city - he worried it might raise anti magic sentiments. There were already plenty of protests - the angel's presence had leaked and some small protests had started near the hospital. People begging to be healed, to be saved.

Furcifer shook his head as they took off towards the tower again. It was time to set this right.

Chapter 34

Outside of the headquarters, a small crowd had formed. People holding signs up.

OUTLAW PORTALS PERMANENTLY

KEEP OUR COMMUNITY MAGIC FREE

MAGIC LAWS NOW

Furcifer tried to read all the signs, to see what they were up against. He was sure by now Mary had come outside and reassured them all that they were working in the best interests of the community, that laws would be discussed in their upcoming talks, but to please not disturb the peace for the sake of their neighbours. The protest was quiet, without any yelling, though they were talking to passerbys. Some mages had come outside to watch the protest, but security seemed to be keeping things at bay. Community goodwill, and all that, words which Mary used. It meant they could not be seen to offend the protesters or any people without magic, really. They drove to a back entrance and unloaded everything.

Gareth looked up as they carried the bags of magic supplies in. "Awesome! Thanks!"

"You could have come along to help carry." Furcifer said.

"I've been working on the spells." Said Gareth, not letting the sass get to him. "I think I have it sorted, we can go tonight but it will be tight. Tomorrow night would be better so I could make sure everything is in order, but..." He shrugged. "I'm guessing tonight is the night."

"I would say so." Said Furcifer. "We need to finish this as soon as possible." Outside, he could vaguely hear the protesters, but it was a dull rumble.

"Alright." Gareth looked over and smiled a little. "That works out for me! I'm so excited to try this! You know what it means if this works?"

"That you started a portal...?" Furcifer looked over.

"No! The first interdimensional portal!"

"That's what I was going to say." Furcifer sighed.

Gareth grinned, his face lighting up. "It will take a

while, though. The spell isn't too long but we will need to draw a circle of protection."

"You think we'll need it?" Furcifer asked surprised. "I mean..."

"We don't know what's on the other end." Gareth said. "I read your notes on what Kaoru said. We don't know where the portal will come out, so we need to be careful. We may end up two meters from the castle, we may end up in a forest, and Kaoru doesn't look like the type who can protect us from whatever the angelic equivalent of a wolf." Gareth looked over and snorted.

Furcifer sighed. "You may be right there." He said. The circle would also keep anything from getting through to this world. Not to mention keep them safe.

"And we'll need to eat before we do this. It'll take a while." He nodded. "The portal isn't going to be there instantly. It needs a while to start and then we need to stabilise it."

"Alright." Furcifer said. This sounded complex but Gareth seemed to have the materials to back it up. "So there's no way to find where this portal comes out?"

"I'm trying to let it come out into the town near the castle. It seems to be the best location." Gareth tidied up his notes as best he could. The empty desk had quickly accumulated new papers, new jots and sketches.

Furcifer looked over it, smiling a little. There were sketches, drawings. Things based on the notes he had handed to the man. It was sweet to see the man theorise about how it looked when he would go in only a few hours. It was almost twilight at least.

"You're coming with us right?" Asked Gabrielle.

"Of course!" Gareth looked over. "I want to see this happen." He was so excited, already packing up a backpack with the notes.

"Alright." Furcifer nodded. "We'll need lights, paper, pens... And a lot of commuting beads."

"I'm not sure they'll work in another world."

"They're not based on remembering or knowing the location. Theoretically they should work." Said Furcifer. "It's better than having no way back at all."

"True. Did you contact Aiden about coming here?" Gabrielle asked, looking over to the other.

"Yeah. He said he'd be here after closing." Said Furcifer. "And Twitch is hitching along as well. He might be able to help us with the magical parts."

Gareth nodded. "Yeahh... He's good with the old languages. I wish I was that good with them."

"Only because he was there to use them." Shrugged Furcifer. "But you're going to be there at a giant moment, you know. The first transdimensional portal."

"Yeah..." Gareth smiled a little sadly, but soon turned away to continue working on his magic spell.

Furcifer could see something was bothering the boy, but he didn't want to push it. He needed his cooperation and whatever it was, it was probably going to come out either way. It was hard keeping secrets in a place like this. Magic had a way of making one reveal their secrets.

Furcifer looked around. It was a chaos, honestly. The chance that this haphazard situation would work out for the best was a long shot. But it was all they had and they would have to make it work somehow. He shook his head. Gabrielle was helping Gareth mix potions. Twitch and Aiden were on their way here. If any crew was going to make this work it would be them. He was proud of how far they had come. Aiden had updated him on the angel's condition throughout.

"We'll do it in here, less chance of the magic being detected." Furcifer decided. When he had spoken to Aiden, Kaoru's arrival spots had all been in private residences which were too risky, or in the open. Too risky as well.

"But what if our wards interfere?" Gabrielle asked.

"The effect should be limited. We can do it in my penthouse flat, I removed all the wards to redo them and we'll be high up." That always helped any kind of magic and it meant that if someone were to come try and stop it they would have to get past security and do all the stairs up – Furcifer's security system could be setup to disable the elevator if they tried to go up to the penthouse. That would keep anyone busy for a while. They would not tell anyone outside of the present company to make sure that nobody could be talked into giving the information. Furcifer especially felt for Joe – the man had been forced to give up information and had been used magically already. No, that council would no longer do any harm to the people of this building. He would make sure of that. It did mean Aiden would have to bring Kaoru along. He texted the man and hoped he hadn't left yet. Leaving Kaoru on his own seemed to be giving him the chance to slip away.

"Alright, then maybe we should move this party upstairs already?" Asked Gabrielle. "I wouldn't want anyone interrupting us."
She was right, Furcifer realised. This floor wasn't as secure as anyone who lived on this floor could easily eavesdrop.
"Alright." Furcifer said, opening up his bag. "Let's get everything packed away."

He looked over. It was not far but there were a lot of fragile bottles and volatile powders to transport. After carefully packing everything away he moved to the elevator, jabbing the button and waiting for the elevator to stop.
Gareth lagged behind, pushing the most volatile parts of the spell on a cart - some liquids which weren't to be mixed just yet, spell books and pages in carefully arranged positions to align the drawings on them.

As the elevator opened, Furcifer spotted Twitch, Kaoru and Aiden in it.

Kaoru looked up. "I am here under protest! I would have preferred the stairs." The angel said, indignantly. He had hurriedly dressed in jeans and a t-shirt, looking too big on his frail frame.

"Going up?" Aiden asked. "Thought you would be at your penthouse, so we were going to take it up to the second last floor then do the stairs up. We brought him along..."

"There goes my best security measure." Furcifer huffed, getting in and arranging people to the side enough to let Gareth push the cart in.

"There we go!" He sighed relieved. "I think we can all fit... "

"Now let's hope the elevator doesn't get stuck." Twitch looked up nervously. The elevator was cramped - they were all standing around the cart and trying to not breathe too deeply as they stood arm to arm.

"Twitch, what have I said about jinxes?" Said Furcifer, looking over. He really did not want this to go wrong. Luckily, the doors slid shut smoothly and the elevator started humming as it made its way up.

"See, nothing to worry about." Twitch shrugged.

Right between the last two floors, however, the elevator shuddered to a halt. The emergency lights went on, and an eerie quiet reigned. Not even the soft hum of the central hub resounded.

"Crap!" Gabrielle reached for the cart to stabilise the flasks before grabbing the emergency phone. "Nothing. They must have turned off the electricity."

Aiden sighed. "That would be fast. You sure it is them already?"

"Yeah." Furcifer took a deep breath. "We'll do it here. We cannot be sure that by the time the power goes back on they won't have someone at every floor. Including the penthouse." He licked his lips. This was bad. Closing his eyes he tried to listen to any kind of sound outside of the elevator. Slowly but surely, he heard the noises of people running around, slamming doors.

"Yup. We're doing it here." He decided, nodding his head. "Enough room?"

"Not by a long shot but when has that ever stopped us?" Gareth grinned and took a deep breath. He inched the cart towards the door and started drawing a circle of protection around the group, chanting a simple spell to protect them from any harm that came through. While stepping into the angels' world might dispel all of their magic, it didn't mean the opposite was true. Something rushing through the portal from the other end would have to be contained until they could figure out how it reacted to this world. They knew little about the animal and plant life over there. Not to mention a single thing out of place, without natural predators, could undo an entire balance, carefully arranged through years and years of natural selection.

"What's next?" Furcifer scooted to let the man behind him. Gabrielle did not seem to like this - she had her arms crossed and was trying to make herself as small as possible. He vaguely remembered she did not like small spaces, and this was already tight for three people - let alone all of them. He looked over and took a deep breath.

"It'll be fine. Just.... Take deep breath and focus on the portal for now. We'll be out of here in no time." He touched her arm briefly and then turned to Gareth when he started speaking.

"Well it will take some time - " Gareth shut up when Furcifer raised an eyebrow at him. "Like no time at all. Before dawn. Easily." He said, shrugging a little and making a face back.

"Oh Gabrielle, can you start mixing the blue and green please? Just pour the blue into the green and stir slowly with the wooden spoon thingy." He said, brimming with energy at the idea of this.

"Twitch! Please keep an eye on the maps." Gareth said, looking over to the page. "If anyone shifts them we may lose a part of a spell we need to do. We don't want to end up in Kansas."

Twitch nodded, carefully weighing down the pages with discarded and unused potion bottles.

Gareth nodded, thriving in the tight spaced hustle. It was nice to see him come to life like this after his almost depressed time doing nothing when his projects had been put on hold. Kaoru was chatting to the young mage vividly, pointing out spell issues and notes which would be useful to make it even more handy. The two got on in a strange way... He just hoped that Kaoru wouldn't try to bed the younger one.

Gabrielle focused on pouring the liquids, slowly pouring one into the other. It was a painfully slow and delicate task, which seemed just fine for her right now. Furcifer didn't think she wanted to think very much about being stuck in a small elevator with an experimental portal as the only way out. Aiden and Twitch poured over the spell work, reading through it and correcting any errors where necessary. Furcifer didn't dwell on it – he really didn't want to imagine there could be errors in this spell that could not be caught in a quick reread. He peeked over to the pages, but soon had to retreat, as the two went through it in a pace too fast for him to read everything. All he could do for now was wait, and trust in their ability to pull this project together. He took a seat and leaned his head against the wall.

Chapter 35

"Hey, wake up!" Gareth was crouched down by Furcifer, gently shaking him.

Furcifer let out a groan and opened his eyes, vaguely remembering the last time a youngster had woken him up. Long story short, it was usually a bad omen.

"I fell asleep?" He wondered how he'd managed that in this small a space. He'd had to lay his legs under the cart.

"Seems so yeah." Nodded Kaoru, looking over. He looked a bit nervous.

"I wish you'd told me you'd do the portal here. I would have said a proper goodbye to my family."

"Your family is in the other world, Kaoru." Furcifer said, stretching out and getting up. He was not going to coddle the boy – they had work to do. The sooner the angel got home, the better for everyone.

"We're about to start the portal." Gareth said. "We're going to need your help."

"No matter how much we would have loved to let you keep sleeping, we kinda need you for this." Gabrielle looked over, holding a glowing flask in her hands. "I don't even get how you managed to sleep through all of this."

"Sip this." She took a demonstrative sip of it herself before handing it over to Gareth next to her, who did the same and then passed it around. By the time it got to Furcifer, the mage made a face, wiped the top of the bottle and sipped it.

"What's that do?" Asked Furcifer as he handed the bottle to Kaoru, who just sniffed it.

"It's a tonic to keep our magic levels high as best as possible." Gareth said. "We might be there for longer than we expected and I'd prefer we're all as close to a hundred percent as possible. Kaoru, you shouldn't need it." He took the small bottle back from the man and corked it, putting it in a bag he handed to Gabrielle.

Gabrielle slung the bag on and took a deep breath, already raring to go.

"Smart." Furcifer had to admit, clearing his throat. That stuff had tasted vile, but it woke him up right away.

The bitterness dried his mouth out a little. He took a deep breath through his mouth to try and clear out the taste.

"So are we spelling it all yet?" He joked. The atmosphere in the elevator was tense, tired. The nap he took had probably been the best accidental decision he'd taken all day.

"Yeah." Gareth cleared his throat and handed out pieces of scribbled on paper. "I tried to write as neatly as I could. Go over it, see if you can read it." He said, looking over.

Furcifer mouthed the first few lines and nodded. "Good enough." He said, taking a deep breath. The nerves were rising up now - he really had not imagined it would be this tense after all - but he was happy to know it was going okay. They hadn't needed his help and he'd rather have an extra mage there than to go in with too few resources.

Gareth added the last few touches to the circle of protection. People shuffling around had dulled the lines in places so they had to be redrawn, and after checking again, he added some extra symbols for protection. At least someone seemed to know what they were doing, Furcifer thought, looking around.

"So remember, once we get through we cannot use any spells we would not use in any unknown environment. No teleports, no vanishes, nothing." Said Gareth. "Do remember the list of authorised spells!"
"What list?" Furcifer called out over the growing mumbling of people scrambling to finish the spell. They were practising, trying, vocalising, ramping up the energy. They would have to pronounce the spell as clearly as possible, no errors, no hesitations. Their energy would be channelled together, strengthened, in unison. One stumble and the entire spell would fail, or worse, backfire. He took a deep breath and read over the notes again, trying not to feel nauseous. This was quite the responsibility and their group was not used to working together. Sure, he knew Aiden, Aiden knew Twitch, Twitch knew Gabrielle but there was no love lost there, Gabrielle knew Gareth and they all knew Furcifer. He sighed and licked his lips. "I'm good."

"You read the entire thing? Back and front?" Asked Aiden, looking over. "You always forget the back."
"Even the back, Aiden." Furcifer said, before shaking his head. "So when do we start?" He looked to Gareth.
"Seven minutes. At that point the potion will be not be at its strongest yet, so it'll allow us to use more energy. And then we skip town." Gareth grinned, too excited about this. Good, Furcifer didn't want to see him worried any longer. Maybe the resignation was faked - but he didn't want to deal with the boy's issues.

The minutes crept by. The emergency lighting in the elevator flickered, but Gabrielle quickly launched a light spell to keep them all in the light. With a sigh he looked back down to the spell and focused. It almost came to a surprise when Gareth piped up.

"Right. Ten seconds. Ten, nine, eight..." They carefully had to synchronise, make sure the spell started at the same time. If someone was off by even a second it would throw off the whole flow and not obscure any mumblers very well. Oh he could foresee a few of them stumbling over the ancient words. Even with the efforts Gareth had made to make the spell as modern as possible, there were just some concepts the new magic books had not translated into a modern version yet.

"Three.. Two... One... Go." He started reading the spell, confidently. Thank goodness, everyone had started at the same time. It was easy for Furcifer to focus on reading when everyone was reading at the same pace, the harmony resounding in the small metal elevator. The spell started a small, lit vortex which slowly widened. By the end of the spell it was about fifty centimetres in diameter.

"Now what?" Furcifer whispered.

"We grow it." Aiden said. "This is where you plundering half my store comes in handy." He took one of the bottles and started splashing the portal, singing parts of the spell again where necessary. As he did, over the course of the next hour, the portal stabilised. Slowly but surely, the portal grew large enough to let through a grown man.

Gareth sighed relieved, coming close to making a cross but stopping himself.

"Alright. Now we wait."

Kaoru took a deep breath, smiling as he looked through the portal.

"I can see my house from here." He quipped.

Furcifer snorted. Seemed like the angel had picked up a very human sense of humour.

Gabrielle piped up. "Wait for what?" She was eyeing the portal as if she would jump through without a second thought. Being cooped up like this really did not make her happy.

"We need to make sure it's stable. Without that certainty it could cut an arm off as soon as we try to go through." Gareth said. "We need to give it at least ten minutes to stabilise fully."

Furcifer groaned. Holding open a portal for that long, even a normal one, was draining. This one would take most of their magical energy and possibly even create a magic-drain nosebleed or two. He looked around. Aiden looked ok. As a general mage, he had the best magic efficiency of them all. He had his specialities which cost him a little less magic than the rest, but most magic didn't cost him much because he had some affinity with all kinds of magic. Gareth would be great - his studies of portals and continued use of them had made him a champion at keeping portals open. His current record was keeping a transatlantic portal open for twenty five hours before finally succumbing and closing it. In that time, three hundred people had stepped through, to the other side, enjoying a cheap and super easy trip to the other side of the world at almost no cost. He'd done the event as a charity thing and gotten himself the first magic world record with that one. No, Furcifer didn't worry about him in the slightest.

Gabrielle was rattled - her nerves were shook from being in a closed space for so long, but she was a disciplined mage. She could last an hour, easily.
Twitch was the wildcard here. Sure, he was experienced and powerful, but he never really did any long term magic. He never even really did portals for that matter. But so far, he looked determined and energised. Time would tell. He took a deep breath and focused on keeping the portal open, trying to peek through.

What he saw almost made him lose focus. Just like Manon had described, the village was small and wonderful, beautifully decorated and rustic. There was no sign of electricity but the magic hung thickly in the air. The air coming through the portal was fresh and clean, and he could spot Gabrielle closing her eyes, most likely trying to use that fresh air trying to convince herself she was not stuck in an elevator.

After five minutes, there was a sudden sound. The elevator – it had not been started up. No, it was a more sinister creak, a sound that did not predict a happy ending.

"The elevator safety mechanism might be giving in." Whispered Gabrielle. She could be right there. The elevator would usually be safe for a long time, but with all these people and equipment... they were probably a bit over the weight limit.

"Right, enough waiting." She hurled herself through the portal, before looking around and gasping.

"It's fine! Come through!" Her voice sounded far off, almost hollow.

"Oh..." Aiden looked through it and nodded, before stepping up. Furcifer could tell this was painful for him. He had to do this, and risk never seeing his child again, or his lover. Still, he stepped through. Kaoru just sauntered through, not even bothered by the fuss others were making.

Twitch stepped through after taking a deep breath and walked up to Gabrielle, making sure the group stayed together. Gabrielle tried to take his arm, but he violently flung it off and took a step to the side.

Furcifer looked over to Gareth. "You should have been the one to step through first." He sighed, feeling worried the man had been left behind a bit.
"No thanks. That's fine." Gareth said. "You go on." Just then, the elevator shuddered again.
"You go." Furcifer said. "The elevator is going to drop at any moment. And we don't know where it'll go."

The council could be manipulating it to open at the next floor. Or it was just failing and it would fall straight to the ground floor, crushing anything and anyone inside it.
"No." Gareth shook his head. "If I go through all magic will be lost."
"Not all magic!" Furcifer huffed – before realising. "You mean the long time change magic." He added softly. "Shit." He should have guessed there had been a reason why the teen had been so eager to work on magic that would change one's body permanently.

"That – you were a minor at the time. You weren't supposed to use it. No body altering before twenty one." Furcifer said softly. "That rule was made for a reason."

"That's easy for you to say. Oh god." Gareth croaked as the elevator started moving. Slowly, it slid a meter down. Gareth clung to the handrail so hard his knuckles turned white.

"Gareth. I will throw you through." Furcifer said. "If I have to choose between losing you or the portal..." The elevator croaked, as if to prove his point.

"I don't want to die." Gareth closed his eyes and rushed through the portal.

Furcifer sighed relieved, until the teenager's weight had left the elevator, sending it falling down. Furcifer was thrown clear of the portal as the elevator gained speed. The noise, the speed, it was dizzying.

"Fuck!" Luckily, the portal was moving as well. There was still a chance. He braced himself and pushed himself off, throwing himself against the side wall. He banged his head hard. It was hard to see the portal now – he was dizzy and some blood got into his eyes. The portal was narrowing and had grown opaque, but it was still in its place against the wall of the elevator, moving with him. He was running out of time. He took a deep breath and pushed himself off using the handrail. His hand thrust through the portal and he felt someone clinging to him, pulling him through. It gave him strength - whoever had gone through was safe. He regained his footing and jumped, falling through the portal just as he heard the elevator crash. A few deep breaths later he opened his eyes. His foot was in pain - he looked down to see a bloody wound where the toes of his left foot should be. His head was still spinning.

"The portal collapsed. We couldn't concentrate on keeping it open." Aiden looked over him, taking off his sweater and using it to bandage the wound. "Are you okay?"

"What- " He shook his head. "I'm - it hurts." He hissed as he tried to flex his toes, only to find pain. Moving his head was a Herculean task.

"Big baby." Gabrielle mocked, but he could hear some concern in her voice. She took some potions out of her bag and gave him one to drink. "Can't promise you your toes will grow back but that should keep you on your feet, if you'll excuse the pun." She said as he gulped the potion. His whole body seemed to pulse and glow with warmth, replacing the pain. He shook his head.

"Alright. Everyone okay?" He tried to sit up and take inventory. He knew the bitter taste of those herbs. For about an hour the pain would be gone, but it would come back with a vengeance. He let Gabrielle dab at the wound on his head as he peered around.

Gareth nodded. His face was now distinctly rounder, as well as his hips. The stubble on his face had vanished.

"It's fine, Gareth. We'll be home soon and you won't need to leave your room until you can do those spells again." Furcifer promised him. "No use making you wait until you're twenty one now, huh." He tried to smile, but he was still pulsing with pain.

Gareth looked up, before looking down and nodding briefly. It was not a happy nod, but he was just glad not to have lost a young, promising mage.

Kaoru looked around. Now that Gareth seemed to be down, he had taken charge.

"It seems we're on a hill just near the town." He said, looking over. "It'll take ten minutes to walk there, just about."

"I'm staying here." Furcifer sighed. "I'd rather keep my wits about me rather than force myself to walk and end up exhausted and in more pain." Plus, he could feel the atmosphere's effect on him – he was already growing tired faster than usual.

"Alright." Kaoru said. "You can all stay here, if you wish. I will make you a portal back and you can go. No big deal." He promised. Being here seemed to do him good – he was gaining strength from the magic around him and his face got some colour as he paced around. Not bad for someone who had been shot in the stomach mere weeks ago. Furcifer nodded.

"If you can do that, yeah. Gareth can help me get home." He nodded.

"I need to go to the castle first. Make sure the council is not sending more people through and if so, make sure they back off. I'll send Mammon back with you if they are not letting up."

Gabrielle nodded. "Yeah. One of us can come with you to make sure nothing happens to you?"

Twitch nodded. "I will. I have the least to lose if they arrest me or whatever."

Gabrielle groaned. "That's not what you should be worried about. I'm technically the one without a family and I can fight properly. I'm also the one who looks the least natural." She took a deep breath. She could probably pass for a halfling, Furcifer realised. Not all of them had wings.

Twitch looked over. "Alright. Alright."

"Not hard to talk you out of that one huh?" Furcifer said acridly, realising he would care if Gabrielle didn't return. "What if you don't return, though? I'll be running the faction on my own. Not something I look forward to."

"Oh cry me a river. Find a successor then. There's no reason you cannot manage the faction. Just... be good with it. That's all you need to do." She shrugged and put the bag of supplies down.

"I'll come with." She arranged her top and sighed. "You guys stay here, catch your breath." She nodded, taking Kaoru's arm and taking off before anyone could protest.

Finally regaining his wits, Furcifer called after them. "Ask about the Book of Dreams!"

Chapter 36

Furcifer watched them until they disappeared behind the walls of the town and shook his head. He just hoped she would be okay. A few of the others wandered off, but he'd made sure they stayed within line of sight. But the idea of going foraging... It was too tempting.

"So what do we do?" Aiden asked.

"We wait." Furcifer looked down at his injured foot. The pain was fading a little but he really would feel better being at a hospital. Perhaps they would have been able to save his toes with prompt attention. Perhaps they wouldn't have. He supposed it didn't do to dwell on it.

Aiden sat down next to him and looked over to his foot. "How's it feel?"

Twitch and Gareth had gone down to the village, cloaked up as if they were travellers. From the fact that there had been a few pieces of fabric big enough to pass as cloaks in Twitch's bag, he could have guessed the man had planned a visit to the town.

"It's okay, really. It doesn't hurt anymore but every time I try flexing my toes, nothing happens."

"Can you imagine the cleaner having to clean up that elevator? Finding like your broken shoe and some toes."

Furcifer couldn't help but laugh at that image. "Yeah. I'm sure the cleaner will hate me even more." He laughed. His feud with the cleaning staff everywhere had gotten him in trouble many times.

"So you think she'll be fine?" Furcifer asked, nodding towards the castle.

"Yes." Aiden sighed. "I don't know her that well, but she seems to know what she's doing. She carries herself... well. Like a con artist. Don't give me that look. I used to be one." Aiden sat back and looked around. In the distance, Furcifer could see two figures approaching. After a tense moment, he recognised them.

Twitch sat down with them, abruptly ending the conversation.

"It'll get dark here soon." He said. "Funny how it doesn't feel like time is moving differently here."

"Yeah." Aiden nodded. "Your body just... Adjusts. Much

faster than you would think. Like with jet lag, only it doesn't have to force itself to sleep."

"Sounds about right. I'm already tuckered out." Gareth laughed and shook his head. No way he was going to last here very long. "This is exciting though! I found dragon scale, three kinds of seed we don't have on earth." It seemed to have been a good opportunity for the other to take his mind off.

"Not what I thought crossing into another world would be like." Furcifer had to admit. He'd hoped he could walk into the town, meet people, talk to them. Not lie here uselessly while Gabrielle did all the work, though that was pretty much on par for the course with him. He sighed and closed his eyes. Maybe they could return one day. He really wished that next time it would be a more pleasant visit. But for now, avoiding a war was a good start.

"How long has it been?" Twitch asked nervously. The sun was starting to set in the distance, casting long shadows.

"Almost an hour. I think. I'm not sure our clocks can be trusted here." Aiden checked his watch. The digital watch was usually pretty magic proof, but whether it was following time as it was going here or at home, he could not tell.

"Someone's coming!" Gareth said, shuffling closer to the group.

In the distance, three figures appeared. From this distance, all they could see was that one did not have wings. Hopefully, that is Gabrielle, Furcifer thought, forcing himself to sit to track the approaching figures.

"Is that...?"

"It's Gabrielle." Twitch confirmed. "She's with Kaoru and a third I don't recognise. Looks like some kind of guard or warrior." He reported, looking from the approaching figures back to Aiden and Gareth and back. There was no doubt about it, they were approaching in a steady but leisurely pace. Hardly running to arrest trespassers on their grounds.

Kaoru arrived first and gave a little wave, dressed in a spring green robe with silver embroidery.

"Glad you took the time to change." Furcifer said dryly. "Who is the redhead?" He nodded to the guard like character, who had bright red hair and black leathery wings. When Furcifer focused on them, however, he saw that they were feathery wings, but covered in a layer of leather.

"Mammon?" He raised an eyebrow. "A general coming to meet us."

"Coming to reassure you you will be safe when you leave." Mammon said, trying a smile. Furcifer recognised a fake smile when he saw one – he had faked plenty of them. Still, the man seemed calm and honest. He was reassuring, even if he carried a big sword. The accent was very noticeable, but his words were clear.

"Alright. I'm ready to go when everyone else is. Have you recalled your council?" Furcifer asked.

Kaoru sighed. "We cannot reach them. So we'll be coming back with you. We have your version of commuter beads so we can make our own way back." Mammon said.

"So that's why the big sword." Sighed Furcifer. At its mention, Mammon clasped the handle.

"Just a precaution." The general said.

"They have gone rogue at this point." Kaoru sighed.

"Now that the king is safe they should not be doing any of this." Mammon added with a nod.

Kaoru nodded. "I take full responsibility for that. But at this point I just want to stop them before there are any casualties."

Furcifer nodded and nodded at Twitch to help him up.

Twitch rushed over dutifully and helped him to his good foot. Furcifer rested his weight on the heel of his other foot, just trying to stand without putting his full weight on the other man for now. Even that was a struggle. And getting up made the blood rush to his head as he was hoisted up quite quickly.

"Let's go." Gabrielle nodded to Mammon, who easily opened a portal back to the tower's lobby.

Twitch helped Furcifer through first, putting him down on the couch there. He took a deep breath and looked back to see Gabrielle and Gareth coming through second, with the teenager barely held back from vanishing to his room by Gabrielle.

"We need to make sure it's safe." She whispered to him. Gareth nodded, but he did not look happy about it. Gabrielle let him sit down next to Furcifer.

Lastly, Aiden came through, looking very relieved. He moved to the group on the couch.

Gabrielle nodded. "Right. Me, Mammon and Kaoru can go find the council to make sure they leave."

"That will not be necessary." A voice, almost unearthly, resounded through the hall.

Furcifer felt the hairs on the back of his head stand up. He had felt that aura of magic before, shortly before being attacked in the tower. Now that he didn't have his back to the source, he could see it was the accumulation of the magic field surrounding three men, dressed in inconspicuous sweaters and pants. This was disappointing, he had hoped for long robes and hoods. But this was almost scarier, they could have been in the background so many times and gone unnoticed. They could have asked him for directions or stood in line with him when he went to get lunch. He shivered and tried to take them in as best he could through his blurry vision. He reached up and crumbled some of the dried blood out of his eyebrows.

The middle one was the oldest, with silver and white hair pulled back into a low tail and a well-trimmed beard. The one next to him was dark brown haired, with a hooknose and features not unlike the older man, looking alike enough to be his son. The third man looked unlike both of them and seemed to be the lowest ranking one in the group - he kept his head down and didn't say much. There was definitely a thick cloak of magic around them, hiding wings and strange features.

Kaoru walked up. "Cerberus. I am ordering you to stand down." He said, holding his head up. "I have returned to the castle and reported to the council. You are acting against the interests of the court."

The men laughed. "You are acting against the interests of the court, Kaoru, leading a double life here! You raised a child here which you did not mean to bring to court. You risked the monarchy!"

"Enough!" Kaoru bellowed, louder than Furcifer believed his little body could be capable of. "That's enough, Cerberus. My life at court is my own business, as is my life outside of it. You are merely there to make sure the kingdom is run in a sustainable and honourable manner and it is!"

Cerberus laughed. "You let half breeds guard you and have not yet taken a wife!"

"Mammon. Please place these three under arrest. And Pippin, I am disappointed to see you on this man's side."

The young one looked up briefly, then looked away again. "I'm sorry, your highness."

"If you come home with us now, you will be pardoned and possibly even return to your duties in the halfling guard." Said Kaoru.

The youth seemed to consider it, looking over his companions before shuffling over to Kaoru and falling to his knees. Kaoru briefly touched his head and then whispered something to him which Furcifer could not hear. The young man nodded and rushed through the portal.

Kaoru took a deep breath. "It's just you and your son, Cerberus. The council is too busy deciding where the feast to make up for missing Summerfest will be."

"Then I will alert them to the fact you have a son." Said Cerberus. "We were almost at war with these savages because of your carelessness."

Kaoru balled his fists. "No. He has to decide whether he will take that position. Until he is eighteen he's not fit to make a decision of that scale. That carelessness you are referring to is my personal life, and that is none of your business. You came here and attacked people, a crime for which I should have you tried."

Cerberus backed down a little, impressed by the short man's rage. "So... if he were to make the decision to come to court, you would welcome him as your successor?"

"Yes. Even if my future queen objects." He said. "He would count as my first."

Cerberus nodded. "Very well. But know, milord, that I will use this knowledge against you where needed." He said before walking past him.

Kaoru unclenched his fists and closed the portal after the man's son had passed through.

"Sir?" Mammon looked at him surprised. "You are not returning?"

"Of course I am." Said Kaoru, looking up at his guard. "But I need to see my son first. It's unlikely I will see Mikey again before he turns eighteen and I need to let him know about his choice." Said Kaoru, shaking his head.

"I'd rather not have him make the choice, but he is my son and he has that right." Kaoru looked over to Furcifer. "Medical attention is somewhat overdue for you."

Gabrielle nodded. "I called an ambulance - I don't dare to move him more." The wound had started bleeding again. Furcifer was trying to cling to consciousness.

"Why don't you heal me?" Furcifer asked, glaring over at Kaoru."You heal people, this should be a cinch."

"Yes, but it won't restore your toes. Human medical science is better at restoring those- but magic is aimed at keeping you alive." Said Kaoru. "It would be a stumpier foot and possibly more pain. So unless it turns life threatening, the hospital is your best bet." Said Kaoru, taking the man's hand.

"Thank you for your efforts. You were amazing." He said, as the sounds of the ambulance approached. He walked off towards the door.

"Mammon, I order you to go home." He said.

"Stop him!" Furcifer protested weakly, being held down by Twitch and Gabrielle.

"Ugh, you're letting him just walk out of here?" Said Furcifer. "At least stop that one!" He pointed at Mammon, but the soldier already broke a bead at his feet. As his consciousness faded, Furcifer could see the winged redhead vanishing.

Chapter 37

Furcifer woke up in the hospital. The stiff sheets were tucked tightly around him, his foot on a little heightened stand. He glanced down at it and looked around.

Gabrielle put down the book he was reading. "You're up." She smiled briefly then reached for his hand. "They didn't manage to save two of your toes. One has been reconstructed. But it seemed a big artery was nicked which meant you were losing blood fast. You almost didn't make it there." She straightened up. "And you have one hell of a concussion." She added.

"Well." He sat up and took a deep breath. "Glad I made it then." He winced as the blanket moved over his foot.

"Like anything can kill a weed like you."

Furcifer snorted. "You look so happy I made it as well."

Gabrielle laughed. Her sullen face never showed much emotion. "I am." She said.

"What about Kaoru?"

"He went to stay with his son for the night before. They had a long talk and he's asked me to enrol Mikey into the Hopefuls. He'll be safest there." Said Gabrielle. "He and Oni move into the school's dorms after the summer break."

"Wonderful." Nodded Furcifer. "So Aiden decided on us?"

"Yes. Apparently Kaoru told him this was the only place she would thrive. I don't know if that is true or not. Who knows, maybe he sees the future. But it changed his mind from the Canutta coven to our school."

"Think the Canutta school would still have had Oni after all this?" Furcifer asked.

"The whole operation has been somewhat hush hush." Gabrielle admitted. "We reported to the authorities while you were out, but they are not charging us with anything. Everything has just about settled down, but the portal ban is still up." She told him. "But we're going to have to restart the law talks soon. This whole angel thing only confirms how important it is we have a strategy of sorts." She looked down at her hands briefly, and Furcifer noticed she'd had a change of clothes. This wasn't just a few hours later than he had thought – it seemed he had missed quite a lot.

"The magic wave hit." Gabrielle added with a smile. "Mikey has magic now. He's good at it. Oni is still a bit young but she might have gotten it as well. We're not sure yet."

"I hope she has." Furcifer nodded. It would have broken Aiden's heart to find that his daughter was not at all magic.

"How long have I been out?" Furcifer looked around for a clock.

"Just a few days. Three." She said. "You hadn't slept much in the lead up and then you lost a quarter of your toes and a lot of blood. You should still be resting." She looked up and put a hand to his shoulder to keep him from getting up.

"Is Gareth ok?"

"Of course. He's hiding in his room and we just send up whatever he asks for." Gabrielle said. "He's promised to organise his notes on the angels and to publish a book for us, within six months. We'd be the first to have any kind of published and verified information about the angels." She was obviously excited.

"So I'm guessing Kaoru went home?" He asked.

"Yeah. Though we had to make sure he had left. It turns out..." She cleared her throat. "He was still quite busy when we went to check."

Furcifer laughed a little. "And with busy you mean he

was banging his girlfriend."

"Yes. It seems he's got quite the libido and well, we had told him he could say goodbye to his family." She sighed and rubbed the bridge of her nose. "He's very human in that regard."

Furcifer shook his head. "I sort of liked him." He had to admit. The man had been uncooperative, friendly to the point of annoying, and secretive, but he felt a connection. They had both acted to keep their worlds safe when it came to it.

"The council fucked off?"

"Yes. There was a lot of explaining to do and we've got an ambassador to the angel kingdom now. I don't think you'll like him but he's level headed and will sit in on the law discussions. In an advisory manner – the angel kingdom is ages ahead on magic regulation and offered their expertise."

Furcifer nodded. It did look like it all ended for the best.

"Now just get some rest. I'll be at the tower, so just text me if you need anything." She stretched out. "I'll bring some pyjamas and books for you tomorrow." She walked towards the door and opened it.

Manon was standing just outside of the room, looking up from the phone in her hands.

"Hi." She smiled a little and looked into the room. "Oh, you uh, is visiting hour still going?"

Gabrielle smiled widely. "Of course it is! Come in." She

said with a little smile. "How have you been?" She hugged the woman, who hugged her back happily.

Furcifer just rolled his eyes - he never got these shows of endearment between these two strong women, but he guessed that was why they needed it.

"Hi Manon." He said, breaking up the greeting a bit. "Didn't expect you to come and visit."

She smiled. "It's all calmed down a bit, don't you know? We've got a formal event with Kaoru and the new angel ambassador tomorrow. I do hope you can join." She nodded a bit.

"I should be good for that." He said, sitting up a bit straighter now that Gabrielle was not here to tell him to rest.

"It'll be interesting." She nodded. She was fidgeting with her hands - not her usual relaxed self.

"Are you alright?" Furcifer asked. "You look pale."

"I'm fine. She grinned. "Just... worried for you." Her fingers were bandaged up, definitely from nervous picking.

. "Oh, detectives Ellis and White want to speak to you as soon as you feel up to it."

"Oh, I suddenly feel so weak!" Furcifer leaned back dramatically. "Not today, not today. I cannot do it."

Manon rolled her eyes. "Nobody will believe that." She shook her head. "But just rest up, okay? I need to get going soon."

"Yeah." He sighed as a nurse entered.

"You're up. Let's see if we can get you sitting up." She cheerily announced, throwing the bed covers back. Furcifer protest against the loss of warmth by trying to grab the blanket. The nurse, however, was too fast and held a hand out to help him up.

"Cruel and unusual. I like it." Furcifer ignored the hand and pushed himself up to a seat, turning his legs over the side of the bed and carefully touching the ground. It was cold, but he pressed on, firmly planting his feet. He hadn't thought the loss of a few toes would make much of a difference, but it did – he felt the change as soon as he put his foot down. And after a second, the throbbing pain returned.

"Good good. No need for standing yet, you're going to want to keep weight off of that for as long as possible." Said the nurse, motioning for him to put his feet back onto the bed.

"How does it feel?" She started unwrapping the foot to have a look, and Manon looked away.

"Guess that's my cue to leave!" She waved and made her way out.

"'Bye." Furcifer nodded then looked back to the nurse. "Not too horrible. I mean there's a lot of painkillers in my system." He nodded at the drip.

The nurse nodded and smiled. "As it should. It was starting to get infected by the time you got here so you're going to be taking some antibiotics as well." She looked over the wound and nodded. "Not bad."

Furcifer forced himself to peek, but instantly regretted it. The top part of the foot had been mauled and seemed held together by stitches. He didn't venture further and just laid back into the pillows.

"How long until I can walk again?"

"With crutches, tomorrow. Without them, well, that will be a while. Wounds need to heal you know." The nurse tightly bandaged the wound, peeking up to him from time to time to see if he was in any discomfort. It seemed only a minute before she had finished bandaging up the wound.

Furcifer thought about the last few weeks - the hurt that had caused a man to fire on an angel in the first place. A lot of things would need to heal.

"Hang on. It's Thursday right? Thursday the third?" He glanced around for a clock.

"Yes, almost - ohh." The nurse laughed and grabbed a wheelchair from the side of the room. "Come on. You want to join the gawkers, don't you?"

"Hey, he's a personal friend of mine."

"I'm sure, I'm sure." She said, helping him into the chair. Furcifer felt completely ridiculous in his flimsy hospital gown, hair unbrushed. He ran a hand through it quickly, but the amount of knots made him wince and he gave in for the moment.

The nurse pushed him out of the room and into the hallway, positioning him on the balcony which had a view of the entrance. A lot of people were gathered here for this – quite a few of them patients. As the time came, Kaoru entered, this time dressed in simple jeans and a hoodie, wings poking through slits in the back. He was alone, which surprised Furcifer – he would have never trusted humans again in the man's place.

Kaoru smiled a little, looking around at all the people, seemingly taken aback.

One person started to clap, and he was soon joined by the others in the room.

Kaoru just raised a hand. "No, no please." He looked around with a smile. Spotting Furcifer, he nodded at the man and smiled.

Furcifer merely nodded back curtly.

Kaoru chuckled and shook his head, before walking up the stairs, something he had never done before. People moved out of the way to let him through, some touching his wings as he passed.

"I owe a lot to you, my friend." He said to Furcifer, walking over and touching his shoulder.

"Yeah yeah, not enough to heal my toes." He flapped his hand, jokingly.

Kaoru laughed. "I think you would agree some of the people here need my help more."

Furcifer nodded. "I do." He agreed and ran a hand through his hair. "So get to it. Tomorrow the whole world's going to know who you are. Enjoy the semi anonymity."

Kaoru shook his head. "It'll be different alright. But it'll be good for both our worlds." He took a deep breath and looked around the people gathered. Many just seemed to gawk, never having heard the man talk.

"You got my star pupil pregnant." He half scolded the man.

Kaoru nodded. "She told me. I have set up a fund on earth to help provide for children I've gathered." He said.

"Probably a good start." Furcifer looked over. "I guess you should leave you to your work."

"Mmm." Nodded Kaoru.

"One more question. Why didn't you bring protection? I'm guessing Mammon will accompany you tomorrow?" Furcifer queried.

"Because I'm not here as a king. Besides, I'd like to believe people are good still." He smiled and walked back down the stairs.

Furcifer watched him until he was out of sight and the nurse wheeled him back to his room to clear the hallway.

Epilogue

This time, they had rented out better than a hotel meeting room. And as Furcifer was happy to remark, it wasn't up to them to order the food. Luscious trays of food had been put out, with cheeses and cold meats mixed in with angelic food stuffs like fruits and pastries from the other side. It was a fine example of a diplomatic first meeting - there was no real agenda, and the main idea was just to mingle until the next day, when there was an actual schedule.

It was the first day of a three-day summit to set up the basis for a relationship between the dimensions. Tomorrow, Kaoru would start a self-contained portal between their world and his, and there would be some more polite clapping and fancy snacking. Then the ambassadors would do their work as Kaoru and his bride to be left again.

Kaoru smiled as he arrived, having donned a tuxedo to try and show his willingness to fit in. The only sign of his royalty was a green and silver dress scarf he wore over his shoulders. Next to him, a young angelic lady resided. Pearl was about the same height as Kaoru, only a few inches taller, making them a lovely couple. Her platinum blonde hair framed her face wonderfully and her skin was lit up with a golden gown. She was currently fussing over Kaoru's scarf. He laughed and let her fuss, not engaged in any conversation at the moment.

Furcifer looked away from the couple and grabbed a canape. He had mostly recovered from the adventure and he was happy to be here. Gabrielle and he were representing the faction, with Gareth being invited as the portal specialist. The youth looked delightful in a tuxedo, he had to admit, having ditched his bow tie and unbuttoning the collar to show off the many pendants and charms he was wearing. As the boy chatted with a young angel lady who had joined the royal party, Furcifer chuckled.

"The youngsters never change." Said Furcifer.

Gabrielle shrugged. "They are having fun, leave them be." She sighed. "You should compliment my dress." She changed the subject.

"Oh. Sure. That's a lovely red on you."

"Oh this old thing?" She rolled her eyes and grabbed his arm. "So we'll be in talks all day again tomorrow.

Might as well have some fun now." She said and smiled over to him. "You helped make all of this happen, you know."

"Gareth did more than me." He looked away. "I mostly just got everyone in trouble."

"Not untrue." Gabrielle cocked her head to the side briefly. "Ah, Lydia and Twitch!" She dragged Furcifer over to go say hi to the couple.

Furcifer used his cane to keep up with her pace. He needed the aide less and less, but he felt it looked fancy for the night, and because he would be on his feet all night. So far it had served him well.

"Hi!" Twitch grinned, running a hand through his hair. "So tuxedos and everything huh?" He smiled.

"Yes, this is a proper gala." Said Gabrielle. "Mostly to lure everyone here to do the boring stuff tomorrow." She patted at the back of her head, where her hair was coiled tightly into a bun. As a waiter walked over, she grabbed a glass for her and Lydia. Furcifer and Twitch took a glass of the champagne as well.

"To discovering a new world." Said Gabrielle, raising her glass to the light, briefly reflecting the many light bulbs in the chandelier.

"A new world for both our races." Kaoru walked over with his glass of champagne. "Ah, please meet my princess, Pearl." He briefly kissed her hand. "She'll be my queen."

There was a joy in his eyes at that statement which almost made Furcifer gag.

He simply put his glass up. "To a new beginning."

Vade Mecum Series

Furcifer's Pride

Asa's Blessing

Kaoru's Chaos